MW01051936

PARADISE LOGIC

SOPHIE KEMP

SIMON & SCHUSTER

NEW YORK   AMSTERDAM/ANTWERP   LONDON   TORONTO   SYDNEY   NEW DELHI

Simon & Schuster
1230 Avenue of the Americas
New York, NY 10020

First Simon & Schuster hardcover edition March 2025

SIMON & SCHUSTER and colophon are registered trademarks of Simon & Schuster, LLC

For information about special discounts for bulk purchases, please contact Simon & Schuster Special Sales at 1-866-506-1949 or business@simonandschuster.com.

The Simon & Schuster Speakers Bureau can bring authors to your live event. For more information or to book an event, contact the Simon & Schuster Speakers Bureau at 1-866-248-3049 or visit our website at www.simonspeakers.com.

Interior design by Ruth Lee-Mui

Manufactured in the United States of America

1   3   5   7   9   10   8   6   4   2

Library of Congress Cataloging-in-Publication Data has been applied for.

ISBN 978-1-6680-5703-2
ISBN 978-1-6680-5705-6 (ebook)

Dedication: For the elements were dastardly but I did love you, badly.

Thank you. I am now experienced.

And now I know how Joan of Arc felt / As the flames rose
to her Roman nose / And her Walkman started to melt.

—The Smiths, "Bigmouth Strikes Again"

Ταράσσει τοὺς Ἀνθρώπους οὐ τὰ Πράγματα, Ἀλλὰ τὰ περὶ τῶν
Πραγμάτων Δόγματα ♥ ♥ ♥

—Epictetus

What is—"Paradise"—
Who live there—
Are they "Farmers"—
Do they "hoe"—

—Emily Dickinson

PARADISE LOGIC

YOU WANTED THIS

SO VERY BADLY

DIDN'T YOU?

PROLOGUE

THE GIRL

IN WHICH THE QUEST BEGINS WITH

THREE PIECES OF EVIDENCE

Outer lands:
smith + 9th st
F/G,
stefie's
house

The Talia
Laundromat —
where they will
fuck later

Aziz's
House

Paradise
#221

Ariel +
Reality's
favorite
Deli

Medhi's
studio

GOWANUS

Luis'
pest control
office

The mighty Gowanus canal,
The Venice of New York.

Angels! Manna from heaven! The sounds of trumpets!
Meadowlarks, birch trees, milk and honey
Adam created Eve from one of his ribs
And then what she did was that she ate an apple
And then there was a fall from Paradise
And some time after there was a girl
And the girl was from a town called Observator
But she now lived in a forest called Sapokanikan
And she was just starting to become a grown-up
Which meant she was no longer being bornth from a rib
But instead was eating an apple
And it was the golden hour of her youth—
(She was the age of twenty-three)
Headed to a place called Paradise
Which wasn't heaven. She wasn't allowed there anymore!

It was Gowanus

I have to tell you a story first.

13.8 billion years ago. The explosion of a tiny, dense fireball. The accumulation of particles. The accumulation of stars, of asteroids, of galaxies. Suddenly, a big blue rock. Suddenly, a pool of water. Plankton circling the drain. *A plankton you might even say was in the shape of a girl.* The iridium band they would one day call KT. *15,000 years ago.* A deciduous environment. A girl who is in the nude. Brown nipples, hairy navel. A girl who is eating an apple. She sits underneath a tree. She sighs. The apple coats her teeth. She is full. A snake approaches. *Hello, baby,* it says. She smiles. The snake slithers up close to her and he enters. *5,000 years ago.* A land they did call the Levant. A girl who is in sandals, a tunic. A girl who in her satchel has some unleavened bread. She takes a bite, lets it dissolve in her mouth, scratches her armpit. *When we were slaves in Egypt.* It was so hot, back then. At night she sleeps in a tent. Everyone in the tent is a man. Men, men, men, men, men. One morning she finds some stone plates hovering atop a lake of salt. In an ancient script she makes out the words *girlfriend* and *weekly. 800 years ago.* A girl, wizened by the voice of God. Glancing offstage, she winks because there is this thing where the blaze kisses her skin. Glancing offstage, she winks because she is suffering at the stake. She has said some things that she can not take back. *200 years ago,* a shanty of sticks in a settlement they called *the Pale.* A violence where she watches the gendarmerie strangle her father. A violence of watching his eyes pop out of their sockets. A violence of his body on the ground dead, dead, dead. A match cut to a boat. A girl, a boat, a city that they call New York. *This will all be just fine,* she thinks. The weather is cool and the wind hits her face and the whole of the alphabet hangs there in the sky.

If this was their famous bolero, the strings would now scream: *twenty-three years ago/a babe/a girl/twenty-three years ago/a babe/a girl.* Focus your attention on her now, please. More on this in just one moment, please.

All of this is to say that all of this was foretold. That when she finally made it to Paradise, the girl sighed like a baby bird. *Imagine now that the wings are fluttering.* The girl melted into the ground. *Imagine now that in a nightmare scenario the firefighters are late to arrive and you watch your own skin bubble.* Her eyes welled up with tears and her skin turned dewy. *Imagine now that you have woken up in the peach of dawn and you are moist because of the grass.* She started to convulse and thrash. *Imagine now that you are having a seizure because the movie did not warn you before of the strobe effect.*

Due to all of the above, there was some talk of destiny, of a quest. Of jewel-encrusted swords coming out of stones. Of lizards in the desert who are oracles. Of magazines which tell you how to live beautifully. Of powder-blue-suit-wearing cowboys and Chiron transits across the heat of the white sun. Of lessons to be learned that would be so difficult and so true. Inside of the primordial soup of her brain it was all a cacophony. A buzz she could not turn off. A heavy and deep drift of visual snow that said: *Pay attention to this, something really important is about to happen, babe.*

She was calm in her explanation of why there was some talk of destiny. "Billions of years of violence and discovery has led to this moment," she said. "All culminating in something startling and true."

The girl was acting this way for a super normal reason, actually. The reason was that she had met *him*. She had met a man who could unlock the very key to goodness that lay inside of her soul. This is called a boyfriend. If you do not know what a boyfriend is, I will remind you that the main function of a boyfriend is to unlock goodness inside of the soul. When she made it to Paradise (#221) she had finally found a boy she could convince to take on the most noble role of boyfriend. The role of soul unlocker. Or actually, he found her. She was trapped in the bathroom. And he happened to live there, in Paradise (#221).

He was going to be the boyfriend in question.

And when they climbed the stairs to the roof of Paradise (#221), when she looked at him and slapped a cigarette out of his hand to give him a kiss on the lips featuring tongue, she realized that everything was about to change forever. The reason for this was that she was on a quest. A quest that was so great, so bold.

Here is the quest: to be the greatest girlfriend of all time. The very best there ever was. Here is why: because her heart was ready, Jesus Christ, it was so ready. She didn't even know it at the time but it was. She didn't even realize it but she was ready, she was ready, she was ready.

That she would go on this quest was decided from the moment she was bornth. It was a celestial occurrence. The aforementioned billions of years of progress. A unit of time they call 1996. The Hale-Bopp Comet had just begun its dance across the sky, visible to the naked eye for the first time in many thousands of years. *And oh how it stunned.* Sperm fertilized egg. Political figures took office and a man from Arkansas gave them a kiss. Regulators from a clandestine brotherhood called the Securities and Exchange Commission peeled off their jackets after a long day of warding off crimes of the financial sort. The construction of an unimposing brick building, like some kind of hovering disc three blocks away from the dark waters they called the Gowanus. And in the Greater Boston Area, a curly-haired three-year-old boy revealed himself to be a genius of the piano. *We're so proud of you, Ariel,* said his mother, giving him a little kiss.

This was under the sign of Taurus. May. Verdant growth was happening. A nouveau Cambrian explosion of flora 'n' fauna—cork elms, daffodils, lilacs, a bobolink's soprano chirping from a twig. And a loving mother and father in a small town four hours north of that place they called New Amsterdam, Sapokanikan, the Big Apple, New Yawk, New Yawk. And a full day in labor free of drugs. Pain was meant to be holistic and correctly experienced deliciously. A doctor in teal scrubs and a light bulb attached to the safety goggles. The hum of a machine which tells you if your heart is doing good. (It was, it was, it was.) It brayed. It was strong. A soft breeze fluttered in from a picture window and on a slate-colored transistor radio, jazz.

When the girl was bornth it was the afternoon. The doctor with the teal scrubs and the helpful safety goggles was pleased to tell the parents that this baby was, on all accounts, miraculous, perfect, absolutely perfect. They would always treat her this way, the parents. Like a miracle. Because that is how you go on a quest so great, so bold. You are chosen. You experience something as crazy as being loved from the moment you enter the world.

The girl knew about Paradise from a young age. There was *Paradise Island*, which the girl learned about at age seven because there was a day when she had seen a flyer taped up in the window of a travel agency. The flyer indicated that this was a place with waterfalls and seafood and you could sleep on a bed called California King.

There was Paradise Grill, which was one of those American

restaurants where on her plate next to some chicken nuggets there was a child's aquamarine retainer caked in a crusty layer of bacteria that did not belong to the girl nor did it belong to anyone in her party. This was around age ten. This took place in the Southwest terminal in Washington Dulles, Concourse D.

Around age twelve, Paradise was often a juice bar or a store in the mall that sold sparkly green pants.

Paradise could also be a strip club. There were ladies in that Paradise and it was considered polite to put some dollar bills in their panties and give them compliments. Their asses would jiggle and if this was a pleasing sight it was easy enough to tell them they were very pretty. You could also call them sweet lips.

You could say: *I promise to take care of you, baby.*

A disco ball would drop down and the dancers' flesh would ripple and variegate as some songs played. The girl saw just this at age fifteen. She was there with some chick named Kansas, who was a genuine WASP.

Paradise was also a celestial zone wherein there were angels. Heavenly bodies. Girls playing the harp. A white dress with a sash. Milk and honey. Kalamata olives. A prophet-to-virgin ratio of one to seventy-two.

There was no concrete proof that such a place existed. And the girl needed to see something in order to believe it. So this was not a place she had visited yet.

After all: This was a girl who had a low quantitative IQ. This was a girl who could not draw a cube. This was a girl who only learned her lefts from her rights after a principal sent a note home to her parents being like: *Ok, thy child is errant. She Cannot Tell Right From Left.*

Up until the moment she walked up those stairs into Paradise (#221), she wasn't so sure about heaven or angels or any of that. All of that was Figurative. And she lived in the Real—which is to say the Very Much Not Figurative. But obviously everything changed. She became one of those girls with the harps and the sashes. Because it was her destiny.

Of course, all of this really began—the quest to be the greatest girlfriend of all time—because it was the era when one graduates from college and moves to New York and suddenly time is a never-ending waterslide. The girl was so close to doing something with her life. She was sniffing around, looking for clues.

Here's how she'd spent her days before she was rescued from the bathroom of Paradise (#221): She would sit in the garden a block from her apartment and eat figs from the Turkish deli and brush her hair with a plastic comb. Or she'd pet Watanabe, a stray cat of pure Persian who often would prance around her fire escape looking for a snack. Or she'd listen to guys on the subway make comments about the shape of her ass. Or she'd go to see a movie in the theater in the middle of the day and clap her hands when the two characters on the screen locked lips or when the one you least expected saved the day. If she wanted to walk, she had two legs that were deeply skilled in doing this. If she wanted to swim in the sea it was a matter of pumping air in her bicycle tires and slapping on the appropriate suit.

And her skin was so firm. And the clusters of acne on her chin were kind of cute. And her hands were so strong. And she didn't look weathered. And when she smoked a cigarette it didn't make her chest hurt. And if she were to have seven vodka with eggs at a bar with cracked vinyl booths it would not hurt her head the next day. And if she were to kiss someone she did not need to know if they were a genuine eighties baby or if they had a parrot named McSamson Domingo at home. And the main thing that she did was make what she thought was art but were actually just little magazines that she did on her computer about the major issues of our time featuring drawings and collages.

At this stage, the girl had no real ambitions. Prior to the start of the quest, her main goal was to earn three hundred dollars in sales from a zine she made about all of the injuries she had gotten in mosh pits (she was a punk rock chick), going as far as to buy a camera but not as far as to take any photographic evidence. (Evidence has to be Material to be Real.) Another goal was to become a notary public due to its promise of a personalized stamp. Also, she wanted to act in a play. A small-town repertory company would do the trick. This was not the kind of girl who had dreams of the Great White Way.

As you can imagine: there was a lack of financial capital during this era. There was no brokerage. There was no estate. Her finances were fucked. She could have tried to be less whimsical about the flow of coin but it wasn't time yet. To her Stahhndard and Poorzzzz was the name of a chestnut mare, out there, somewhere. Like, in Ireland? When she closed her eyes at the utterance of this phrase the chestnut mare was galloping in slow motion through a peat bog. That was a Holy Grail. The calm of a peat bog. The scent of a chest-nut maaare.

For money, she took what she could get. She was a cashier at the store. If you're wondering how much money she made from being a cashier at the store: it was not enough. If you're wondering how she was able to live on not enough: she was broke as fuck.

Here's the thing. Fais Attention, SVP!!! There weren't many jobs afforded to women at age twenty-three even if you were bright and pure of spirit. Even if you strive to always be clean. Even if everything in your life is done de rigueur. If you were not a cashier at the store, the main jobs were charter school instructor or lady who masturbates on websites to the delight of her adoring fans. The girl was not about to do either of those things.

For now, she needs a name. We must give her a name before she starts her quest in earnest. Because a hero needs a name. Because this will be tragic. Because when you are twenty-three you can fall in love with anyone and this is a terrifying and true thing. Let's call the girl Reality. Reality Kahn. Let's follow Reality on her quest.

Read on, *man.*

VOLUME ONE

REALITY

IN WHICH REALITY SEARCHES FAR

AND WIDE FOR HER BOYFRIEND

ONE

This was a peculiar time. I had to bathe often. I was acting like a child with an affliction. But I was certain that the future would show itself if only my spirit became clean. I needed to have a clean spirit. It needed to be cleansed. The dirty spirit. Cholera of the mind. And Emil's tub was the place to do this—to cleanse.

I was at Emil's house floating in his bathtub while he read to me. Emil was my friend because he was a marijuana merchant. Again: similar to bathing, I smoked the pot to cleanse my soul of any sort of negative properties. There were a lot of negative properties in my soul at this time.

Emil and I met on the train. We were the only two people who were not Hasidic Jews who got off at our stop. Emil looked like a classic punk rock type of guy: jeans with holes, T-shirt featuring a skateboarder clown, music playing at deafening tones. I was wearing an elegant floral chemise that I found in a box that said: FREE! PLEASE TAKE! NO BED BUGS!!!! I was listening to classical music of the most stunning variety at a loud volume on some earbuds I had slipped into a silk purse without anyone knowing, in a deli in one of those neighborhoods where all the babies are named something romantic and esteemed.

Example: Rebecca Stern
Example: Bunny Rabbit Jones
Example: Quanta Contra

As we were getting off the train he said: "Get a drink with me."
And I responded: "I will accompany you to the local watering

hole for the purpose of companionship and possibly sexual intercourse."

Emil lived in an old Tudor that was falling apart. It was right next to an overpass, which was above a highway called the Prospect Expressway. This is known to be one of our greatest routes. This is known to be the Wall of Hadrian of the 21st c. There was a big wraparound porch. It had Tibetan prayer flags and big plants and hand-painted signs that said everyone's political beliefs: Peace Love Unity Respect. All Are Welcome Here. Emil had eight to twelve roommates. It was a cooperative living situation where they all purchased nutritional yeast powder in four-pound bags and all the girls had one long braid and armpit hair, and all the boys had tattoos of iconography like a hippo playing basketball. It was, I guess, Eastern Symbolism. Aesthetically, it was a bit confused.

No one minded that Emil was dealing drugs from the house. Even though it was getting Faustian. Even though there was a severity to the exchanges of goods & services. They gave him reduced rent, on account of the fact that he gave everybody a little bit for free.

What Emil and I usually did is I would send him a correspondence via cell phone informing him that I would like to purchase some drugs, and then I would come over and he would read me magazines while I sat in the bathtub on the second floor. The bathtub was luxurious and claw-footed. This was decadence façon Reality. I would sit there in goggles and a Speedo racing suit. If the tub had been bigger then I certainly would have tried to do some strokes to promote health. Like the front crawl.

We did not have a tub in my apartment. We just had a shower and it always smelled like beans mixed with sulfur. Emil understood these horrors and was merciful. I was depressed by the tenement nature of my residence, but I guess a shower was better than if my only option was to crouch in the sink and let the water turn black. I had seen that happen in some literature. Everyone in the literature was sad.

Emil's reading today was about a famous pop star who was under arrest because of what had happened at cheer camp for incoming college freshmen. He was there as the guest of honor. He was there to perform his famous songs, the very best ones. The girls were there to hone their skills. He invited a few of them—the prettiest and bestest ones— to do something *really fun*. A motel room with a bright pink divan. A tattoo gun that the pop star used to ink his signature above the anal cleft of a girl they all called One of The Twins. Bottles of fine alcohols and baggies of even finer white powdery drugs. The girls got wasted. The girls took off their little white tops and their little blue skirts. The girls all got into bed with the pop star. The girls noticed that the pop star had fallen unconscious in the motel room, this pleasure dome. The girls noticed that the pop star wouldn't wake up. The girls checked his pulse. The girls touched his dick. The girls worried that maybe he had overdosed on the fine alcohols and the even finer white powdery drugs.

After all, a heart can stop just like that.

The girls called the cops, but when they arrived everyone initially was like: we don't want to press charges. The police said furnishing such fine alcohols and even finer white powdery drugs was a criminal offense. But then one of them, who came from a small Southern town where litigious retribution was a local sport, decided the police were right, and besides, she wanted to become so rich. A messy court battle ensued. The pop star pleaded mentally insane and was checked into a small regional rehabilitation center for famous guys who get all coked up, thereby endangering several beloved barely-of-age cheerleaders who went to state school and drove pink Jeeps and gave sloppy blow jobs. *Slurp.*

"Did they really include the details about the Jeeps in the article?" I asked Emil.

"Nah, girl," said Emil, shaking his head. "I'm just extrapolating. Storytelling. You know. Like, I'm adding extra details because I know how it really went down. Intuition."

I submerged my head in the tub water. I did an underwater breathing contest with just me. I wondered how long I could stay down there. Ten . . . twelve . . . a hundred and eighty-seven squared. I wish I could've been the first girl to get her own set of gills. I stroked my very own neck and imagined it all opalescent and algae-covered.

Isn't it marvelous, Reality? Isn't it marvelous in the tub deep blau? That's what I said to the version of myself that was out there on the calmest seas becoming a fish. La mer Méditerranée. I was dreaming, of course, of the island known as Crete—coming up for air only when it was time for, like, some kind of medicinal amaro—letting the diet of these Europeans take its course on my flesh.

I started to asphyxiate because I actually wasn't about to grow some gills. I bobbed back up like an apple in bobbing for apples. It was not time to die yet. I had errands to run. My schedule was packed actually.

"Yo, girl, ok listen," said Emil when I surfaced. "I love hanging out with you and having you take a bath here and all, but you need other hobbies. You have to stop calling me up on your cell phone being, like, 'I wanna use your bath like a mineral spa for tubercular cases.'"

"I need to bathe so my spirit can be clean. My spirit is covered in soot. It is a dirty spirit. And besides, I do have hobbies."

"No, I mean like. You need to like. Go out more in the world. Girl, you know what you need? You need a boyfriend."

"A boyfriend?"

"Yeah, girl. I mean. I think it could be really fun for you," he continued. Emil was talking a million miles a minute! He was in Emil Has An Idea Mode—that's for sure. "Seriously. Yeah. Ok. That's what you need. You need to start letting a guy go take you out for—what's that cocktail you're always drinking?"

"Vodka with egg," I responded.

"Disgusting," said Emil. He was now stroking my thigh.

I had really not given the concept of the boyfriend much thought. It was not a priority for me. I was considered to be highly unusual and extremely sexual. I have to admit that I liked to have a good time.

Pleasantries were a favorite activity of mine. I have to be honest and say that the operative at this point in time was getting my rocks off, albeit nomadically. I was pretty content with the current situation. Only occasionally was I the Apostle Paul, suffahring just like that.

I pressed my hands to my temples. A boyfriend could, I guess, add color to my life as well as provide intrigue. It would certainly be a hobby. It would not be as satisfying as one day being some kind of siren bornth of the global north.

"Ok, well. I guess I'm interested in hearing more," I said. "Where do boyfriends like to hang out?"

"Where do they hang out? Girl, I think you're sexy as fuck and fun, but for serious, you are on some sort of insane-ass trip these days. They're not a pack of wildebeests in the plains."

"Yes," I said, furrowing my brow, "I'm going to need some more intel, about where boyfriends hang out, please."

"Dunno," said Emil, taking the hand that was on my thigh and putting it into my one-piece Speedo racing suit. "Wow, you're so wet. Ha ha. Not just because you're in the tub. I mean your pussy."

"Well, where have you found girlfriends in the past?" I asked, clenching my teeth because of the foreign intruder inside of my one-piece Speedo racing suit. I began to think of Lexy, an ex-girlfriend of Emil's. If I recall correctly, it was on a website where they met. Emil had invited her to see a movie about a world-famous rapist who enchants the world with song, Lexy accepted, and then it was true love for the next three years.

"Well, I mean. It just kind of happens," he said. "Get out of the tub and get naked."

"Happens?" I responded, pulling off my one-piece Speedo racing suit.

"Yeah. Like, you can't make one appear out of thin air. It's called chemistry, Reality," said Emil, taking one of my supple rose-colored areolas and squeezing it like a delightful piece of Bubble Wrap. "Fuck. Get on the ground on your hands and knees like a dog who needs to have a penis in its tiny little pussy. Yeah. Exactly."

I got on the ground like a beloved fido and looked at Emil with googly eyes. Seeing that I had done an amazing job, he spit on his hand and put his penis into the organ, vigorously jamming his wonderful member as far as it could possibly go, which was actually pretty far. He grabbed my hair and said stuff like, "You want this so bad, Reality." And, "You're fucking disgusting. You love being fucked by my cock. I bet you had a fucking lisp as a child. I bet you had occupational issues that made it hard for you to hold a pencil." *Fido, fido, be a fido*, my brain yelped. "Bowwow wow, bowwow. I am a fido as well as a small child," I responded as Emil's cock thrust further inside Reality's organ. "That's so fucked up," said Emil. Then he immediately became Mr. Firehose about the whole thing.

"Did you come?" asked Emil.

"I have had an orgasm every time I have ever had sex," I responded confidently.

But I didn't!!!!! The word boyfriend *was glowing inside of my head via an impressive vaudevillian light display, making it difficult for me to focus.*

We got dressed and decided to smoke from Emil's grav bong, which he had been gifted by a Sikh guy he played "high-stakes poker" with in Astoria. He and the guy were always sending each other marijuana videos on their cell phones. When I looked down at Emil's cell phone I would always see a message that said: LOL JUST RIPPED A FAT 1. And then Emil would respond by saying: "Mashallah, my brother," even though Sikh is not the same as Muslim and also Emil was a Filipino atheist.

Emil took a big hit and then I took a big hit. In a matter of seconds, my brain was cloudy with marijuana and I could not think straight. Emil asked if I was "stoney baloney," and when I said yes, he told me that I was a "good girl." He also told me I needed to stop hanging out in a wet bathing suit 24/7 because it was making the organ "smell nasty, like an onion in a dumpster." I got up and left. I was pretty sure I had negated any soul-cleansing properties by having intercourse and doing bong rips.

I walked out of Emil's house with wet hair and in a bit of a daze. I was feeling really high on the weed. It was like I had marbles rolling around in there. *Click click click.* This is how I imagined the marbles bumping into each other.

The walk was quite short. As I mentioned before, me and Emil lived more or less in the same neighborhood. It was a place that was just a quick bike ride away from Coney Island. To get home, I had to go down Ocean Parkway, past car washes and oil-slick puddles that appeared to have rainbows on the surface. I stopped for a minute to gaze upon my reflection. I liked seeing my face in the puddle, all varicolored. I smiled. It would be cool to one day have a head that is a rainbow. The Rainbow Girl is what I would be called. The Rainbow Girl of Ocean Parkway.

I continued on. I felt bothered by this question of a boyfriend. Would having a special guy around really make me happier? Was this the life purpose I was looking for? What would we even do together? Go to the baseball game? Would he give me a prion disease? Would I wake up in the middle of the night giggling like some kind of afflicted madman?

Ha ha ha ha ha ha ha
ha ha ha ha ha ha
ha ha ha ha ha ha
etc.

The idea of a 2 a.m. witticism felt loathsome, honestly. I was trying to get my eight hours in. I was becoming well. I had some fears about what would happen when I found him. This boyfriend. It was true that

I liked my life. I liked living in my apartment with my roommates above the Benchers store where they sold yarmulkes and other Jewish toys. I didn't have many needs. The main meal I ate was tomato soup and grilled cheese. I made my little zines. I called my parents and said I love you to them and they'd say it back. Then they would ask about City Life and they would tell me that I seemed happy and well-adjusted and I would respond by saying thank you, thank you.

I'm getting off topic and repeating myself. No one cares that I have awesome parents that love me. I'm just some foolish broad with brown hair who just walked out of her friend Emil's apartment. But maybe Emil was right. Maybe I needed a life upgrade. My life was fabulous, but also how long could I go on living a life where I dress like some kind of hobo in 1931? It was romance to be a boxcar gamine but that couldn't be It. I didn't even know how to play the accordion or weave.

I started to imagine this future where I was a boxcar gamine, sitting on a boxcar playing a small ditty on a navy blue accordion, then taking a break from my accordion playing to tend to my loom where a scarf was being made courtesy of my fair hands and fey constitution.

I think part of me wanted more in life than to be itinerant. If I wanted to be a hobo this would be good for me financially. It would solve many of those kinds of problems.

It would be bad because I would seriously get raped by a band of knaves.

This was something I was trying to avoid: getting raped so much. It was hard to avoid this fate. New York City was a place where nefarious individuals got ideas.

Maybe finding a boyfriend would change that. I wasn't sure. I needed a protector from the elements, which more often than not were dastardly. In this situation he'd have to be heavily armed, and I wasn't sure that was realistic given the populace I was drawn to. Guys like Emil had weapons they did not know how to use. I think in general I needed more structure. I wasn't about to get a nine-to-five because it didn't make sense, politically. Also I didn't have any skills? Besides the fact that I was the greatest actress for water park commercials on the Eastern Seaboard. Another skill I guess was being Emil's "cum dumpster."

I had a moment of clarity: Join a league. Take up Mahjong. Consider the lilies. Learn about the Brutalist art form. Look at the Louise Bourgeois in the museum and have a moment of genius. Appreciate free jazz. Play the game badminton. *Batter up, girlie girl.* *Suh-wing battah battah* But then I remembered I was not coordinated. But then I remembered I did not have much follow-through. I had tunnel vision. My vision was marred by elements.

Here was another problem: What would I even do if I found a suitable candidate? Make goo-goo gah-gah eyes and suck their cock? I knew all too well that in true-love situations like Emil and Lexy, the rules were different from when you do casual sexual intercourse.

It is not the same with boyfriends. Just because New York was a city of gentlemen intent on pounding the organ into a fine steak did not mean that they wanted to be my boyfriend. They had a sexual way of looking at me. Crazed eyes. Wagging tongues like a pack of wild, leashless dogs. Dogs running through the night. With boyfriends, there's history there. This is way different from a triumvirate of canine terrorists. You're making a commitment. A boyfriend I have heard is a lifelong commitment. Once you have one you're never the same. You become a girlfriend. This is a fixed identity. I didn't have one of those yet. Being a girlfriend is similar to joining the Franciscans or the Freemasons. Better than badminton, I guess.

I was going to do it. I was going to find a boyfriend.

TWO

I was back at my apartment. Outside, I saw one of the Hasids standing in front of the Benchers store. I nodded my head deeply to him, and he averted his gaze. I believe this was because of his religion. Thou shalt not steal a glance upon the face of Reality Kahn. Fair. I did not have the heart to tell them that I, too, was Chosen! I was La Belle Juive. I, too, had family stuffed into the ovens! They were totally dead!!!!!! Second cousins with names like Esther and Franz had died at the very fisticuffs of evil. He did not get it. Therefore: up the stairs I went. The downstairs neighbors were playing loud DJ music with a fair amount of bass. It smelled of cigarettes. I knew this to be a disgusting habit even though I did deign to light up on certain occurrences. Yuck. I retched loudly to let them know I was back.

My apartment was on the top floor. In it were my two friends Soo-jin and Lord Byron. They were a couple. Lord Byron went by that name because it makes him feel like his life is important. Soo-jin went by Soo-jin because that's the name her parents gave her.

Here's how I met them: it was in college. Back then what I did was act in plays and everyone treated me as though I was some kind of physical or mental disease sufferer. For the record, I had a clean bill of health mentally and physically. Individuals often commented on my normal personality.

Simply Reality. That was me. I had a reputation to maintain. If you pictured a girl with brown hair, a beautiful smile, and shining eyeballs who wears a dress you would say: she's normal and better yet—she has a come-hither attitude.

I met Soo-jin first. Ok, so she was eating some beans on the front porch of her vegan co-op that she and her friends lived in and I said: "I'm hungry, can I have some." And her response was: "Are you that crazy cunt named Reality? I've heard all about you." As for Lord Byron: I met him because he started doing intercourse with Soo-jin after an event called Silent Disco. And then they became boyfriend and girlfriend. And then when everyone moved to New York City just last year at age twenty-two, Soo-jin revealed to me that they were on the hunt for a roommate. Leases were signed. Beds were built. The neighborhood was decided upon due to its close proximity to a specific subway line and a graveyard. It is not interesting. But they are my friends.

I unlocked the door, and there they both were. Soo-jin was knitting something—a sweater, I believe. Lord Byron was just lying on the couch in a moment of repose, being Mr. Oblomov. They didn't really do anything during the day, my roommates. They were just like me. Lord Byron's main job was that he worked for a staffing agency that placed temps. They called Lord Byron by his Christian street name at that job, which was Justin Hopkins Jr. Soo-jin meanwhile worked for an older lady named Gwen who needed help with learning the facts about email.

"I am home," I announced.

There was silence. Soo-jin did not look up from her knitting. Lord Byron did not stop being the hero of the couch. I was being ignored! I felt like a fool and a failure. I thought about stabbing myself with a kitchen knife, but then decided this was not necessary.

"I have a question," I said.

"Hnnnnhhn," said Lord Byron. Soo-jin continued to look silently at her knitting instead of me (Reality).

"A *friend* said I should get a boyfriend because he doesn't think I have hobbies even though I do and I am now looking for a boyfriend. I am wondering if either of you have any suggestions as to where I can go to make myself the most eligible bachelorette possible."

Soo-jin finally stopped looking at her handiwork because I guess I had finally said something interesting to her. "Oh, boyfriend! Yeah.

It would be so nice if you met someone because then you wouldn't be home all the time. No offense."

I took my house keys and dug them into my wrists. I'll show Soo-jin who is home all the time when she has to call 911 because I've slit my wrists!!! Ha ha ha. Oh goodness. I was really being this really specific kind of violent girl today.

"Reality with a boyfriend!" said Lord Byron. "We could go on double dates at that all-you-can-eat Uzbek buffet down the street."

"Double date? I don't even have a boyfriend yet. Where *do* I find one?" I asked, my eyes downcast. How could I think about Tashkent Buffet World in this way?

I felt ashamed for even bringing this up. I could tell they were ridiculing me. In their heads they were thinking terrible thoughts about me and my character. Home all the time. Ha ha ha. Yeah. I'll show you home all the time! I once again eyed the kitchen knife. That would be better than my house keys. *A knife would be a way to go**

"I don't know, girl, a party or something, or you can find one on a website," said Soo-jin.

"You'll remember me and Soo-jin met at a rave," said Lord Byron. "And how lucky we were to have found each other. To have found each other's bodies. I can still feel the way the sun kissed my flesh when I woke up next to Soo-jin for the first time, and how beautiful and new she felt to me. And now every morning when we wake up together she becomes new to me all over again."

"What he said," said Soo-jin. "You just need to be home less often and stop having sex with that guy you met on the F train."

"His name is Emil," I responded, storming off into my room. I could tell when I wasn't wanted.

That night I could hardly sleep. It was like, all of a sudden, all I could think about was boyfriends. I was hot on the case. I was like a beautiful and svelte female detective who had an enormous folding magnifying glass where you can see everything and anything.

I decided to consult some websites for further information.

On a website called iwantaboyfriend.com, I was greeted with a cartoon image of a man who introduced himself as godaddy. I clicked on his image and I was redirected to another website asking for my credit card information. I didn't have one of those. I kept my money in a really safe place (aka under my mattress). *Useless* was the word running through my brain. I slammed my head down on a book. *FAILURE!* was the word that followed the word *Useless.* I wanted to scream. I wanted someone to shove their fist in my mouth so my screams were muffled.

I then consulted a forum where Marly, a girl of fifteen, was asking how she could get a boyfriend at her high school, which was in Des Moines. It read:

I am fifteen and live in Des Moines.

I am looking for a boyfriend. A big guy who will take me for rides in his
 sports car and pleasure my pillowy soft breasts. He will be very rich.

And charming.

And, able to pleasure my pillowy soft boob.

My eyes scrolled down to the comments. Thousands of men were vying for fifteen-year-old Marly's attention. *Ok,* I thought to myself. *I just need to be like Marly, age fifteen.* The men all wanted to be her boyfriend.

I am not so rich, wrote one man, but I would love to take an All American Girl for a ride in my Honda Accord.

Another said: My friends tell me I am like a labrador. I am very loyal . . . I am quite obese as well, but this shouldn't be a problem given how loyal I am To My Woman.

I am in Moldova and I love to sexy with Marly, age 15, said another promising candidate.

I closed my computer. Suddenly the famous song known as the bolero began to play. The strings swelled. I looked around. Forsooth—what was the cause of this stunning music? And the timing could not be discounted. One minute, you are on your computer doing research on how to be a girlfriend, and the next, the sound of oboes, the sound of the cor anglais. Hovering in midair, bathed in a strange yellow light, I saw a magazine. First word *Girlfriend*, second *Weekly*.

The music cut off. A voice inside of my brain shouted: *They first found this text in an ancient era in the form of stone plates, somewhere in the land they did call the Levant. Now it is available for purchase both online and in print. It is now clear that you are ready to embark on a quest so great and so bold. This text will be your aide-de-camp on your peregrinations.*

Ok, makes sense. I was glad to hear that I had been Chosen. And I suppose that I'd take a look at this text that would surely be my aide-de-camp on my peregrinations. Thus: I flipped through the pages. Page after page of how to be a good girlfriend if your special man was a diplomat or a lawyer or a financier. These girls carried parasols and wore fine summer dresses as they disembarked Cessnas and the car called Mercedes-Benz. Glamor. Luxury. Champagne. Spumante. Italiano. Febbraio. This was something I rarely encountered. I was envisioning untouchable decadence. Note to self: *A Boyfriend Could Be A Shot At Opulence Pro Forma.* I decided to read further. *PRO FORMA* was the operative.

HOW TO BECOME A GIRLFRIEND

Hello, female, you are reading this because you are to be recently finding out you have a destiny. And this is a girlfriend. Yes. You are of a young age and are looking for something to do. This is a worthwhile cause. Young men all over the world are in need of your services. Think of all of the petit fours you will make him. And of course, your crystalline eyeballs and taut lips will be considered a beautiful luxury. One does not need to be previously chaste for this task. In our Modern Age it is in fact considered to be an asset to be experienced. You are going to however need a heart which will be open for love.

That is what the article said. This was the path to greatness I was looking for. Everything was so clear. Maybe what you do when you are twenty-three instead of trying to become famous for making art is figure out the perfect yacht to buy your special guy for his fortieth birthday. Or perhaps what you do is check out these restaurants where you can eat Welsh rarebit in a secluded garden setting with a sort of hush-hush policy at the door with regards to child brides and this jeune fille you buy on a website. I reread the words again: *You are of a young age and are looking for something to do. This is a worthwhile cause. Young men all over the world are in need of your services.* They took on a new meaning. Girlfriend was a cause worth fighting for.

Everything was now coming together beautifully. I took out a pen and pad and began to strategize:

BOYFRIEND: How to GET the Guy

1. You can post on a forum like Marly, age fifteen.
2. You can go to the rave like Soo-jin and Lord Byron.
3. You can go to a house party. This is considered a classic tactic.
4. You can go to finishing school in Ljubljana and then at the end an amazing guy will find you because you are a master of embroidery (call toll-free number in GF WEEKLY for further info).
5. Perhaps if you go to the supermarket you can compliment a man on what he is buying and then he will ask for you to be his wife. Saw this one time. But the man was German.

I clicked off my pen and then I plunged my whole body into my bed and fell gorgeously asleep.

THREE

It was time to get spiritual. The camel was being threaded through the needle. It was time to get serious. Grim Premonition: things wouldn't go as planned. Make it positive: true love was to make a resurgence. I had to keep my eye on the prize. I got out of bed and began to pace. I said good morning to Mr. Sun. Mr. Sun said good morning by dappling my flesh with his warmth. I blew out the candle I kept by my bedside to ward off nasty spirits. It was a candle of frankincense. I did seventy-five sit-ups as well as some stretches. I sharpened some of my knives. I had this feeling that being a girlfriend was about being firm in the flesh. And also very skilled at self-defense. I was doing all of this for him—wherever he was. Whatever he was doing. An image of some kind of man eating an egg out of a ceramic eggcup appeared loudly inside of my brain. The learned gentleman would also need to be reading perhaps a paper about the latest deals. The name S&P 500 was reminding me of a chestnut mare. And also the mighty bull. Bull market. Toro toro toro, etc. Killer of Bullz. It was time to find him, my boyfriend.

The first order of business was to go to the various locations where you can meet boyfriends. I had my list, but I needed to consult an outside source. It's called fieldwork—look it up. It's called doing independent research. Leave no stone unturned. No—more extreme—leave no boulder unbouldered. Here's a source worth calling: Emil. I typed in his digits. This was a guy who might very well have additional information as to where I might be able to find a boyfriend. The phone rang twice, and then he answered.

"Girl, you for serious need to stop calling me this early in the morning," he said. "You trying to come over here and help me with this morning wood? I'm hard, baby."

"Emil. This is urgent. I cannot think about sucking your cock right now," I responded calmly, thinking of Emil's cock. "I am wondering where I should go to find a boyfriend. I have been refining my list all evening on the question of the boyfriend and I am ready to begin to execute the strategy."

"*Boyfriends . . .*" he said in an inquisitive tone of voice. I bet he was stroking his famous Emil goatee.

"Yes. Where would you recommend I start my search?"

"I don't know, Reality. It's too early for this. Fuuuuckingchriiist. I told you that you can't find one in thin air. Literally sometimes I'm like: girl, did you learn about social mores from flashcards or some shit? Come on. You're always picking up guys. Haven't you had sex with, like, ninety people? Dudes love a quirky broad with a nice ass. You should be a pro at this. Go to the mall or something. I know you like to go there. Remember when I bought you that hat from Lids?"

I did. It was a disturbing memory.

The mall! I had observed many beautiful couples in love at the mall. The mall was not in a place I could walk to. It involved two subway changes, and then a walk across a very busy intersection where I had once watched a rat die. I watched his guts splatter all over the place as he was pummeled to death by a little red car—a Fiat I believe. It was a disgusting sight, and I thought about it as I prepared myself for the journey ahead of me. It was foolish to buy an Italian car because you are too low to the ground to see one of nature's wisest and most conniving critters, the rat. An appropriate vehicle is a Jeneral Purpose Vehicle. The journey to the mall would be worth it. I was down to risk it all. Even if this involved Bedlam. Oh, it certainly would involve Bedlam. Maybe it was there, in the lower floors of the Atlantic Terminal Mall, that I would see him and I would know he was mine.

I packed a bag for the day. This was crucial. I liked to be prepared for obstacles. I liked to know in advance that if I were to get in trouble, I had all that I needed. In my rucksack, I packed a water bottle, a wallet with my ID, foreign currency from countries like England, France, and Samoa, a pair of sunglasses, a sweater with the name "Reality" emblazoned on the chest, and my favorite knife, purchased from a man I met on a website who promised it would draw blood upon skin contact. Alias: Samuel the Ozone Park Knife Prince. I then found shoes to wear. They were sturdy espadrilles that gave the illusion that I was an austere glamazon, and also provided adequate comfort for the ten-minute march from my apartment to the first of the two trains. I was ready. I looked very beautiful. I even did some mascara on my eyelashes and applied a bit of lipstick to my lips. The dress I wore was a very large T-shirt. It depicted the Tasmanian Devil, thereby proving I was tough.

I walked back into the living room. Soo-jin and Lord Byron were eating some marshmallow cereal and working on a thousand-piece puzzle of a cat who would like to climb a tree.

"I am leaving now," I said to my roommates.

Silence.

"You might not see me for quite some time. I am not sure when I will return. Today could be the day where I find the boyfriend and become his special girl."

"Ok, Reality," said Soo-jin. "Just let us know if you're gonna be back for dinner because the plan was we were going to make, like, a stew or something."

That was a nice thought—eating a stew or something with my two in-love roommate friends. I sighed a happy sigh because it was an image that felt good. I would certainly try to return in time for stew, although no promises were to be made.

"Thank you for the invite, Soo-jin," I said in deep appreciation.

"Good for you getting out of the house!" she said.

Outside of the apartment building, the Hasidic man sat on the stoop. He was smoking a cigarette. This time I waved. He did not wave back. If I were to guess, he was not so much older than me. Twenty-five years old, perhaps. I liked the expression on his face. It was one that seemed intelligent. A scholar of the Talmud. I wondered if he was married or was soon to be married. I wondered what would happen if I were to talk to him. Maybe he would ask me why such a lovely girl such as myself lived in this part of town. Maybe he was curious whether or not I was betrothed. A part of me thought it would be nice to be the girlfriend of a man of God. It wouldn't be so crazy. I could carry his seed and engage in intercourse 'neath a special sheet. But then I thought: No.

I walked away. I popped out my hip. I shook out my hair a little bit. I wanted to give him something to remember. I knew what I was doing. I could really do this. It seemed so possible. I had my charm, that was for sure. I had my spunk, too. And I had my words. I knew that when I saw my future boyfriend, I would know what to say.

On the way to the subway, I felt like I was underwater. I saw many different genres of guys. There were tall guys who looked like string beans. There were shorter guys with a violent look in their eyes. I saw Bangladeshi men sitting at red plastic card tables in front of sweet shops where they were drinking styrofoam cups of coffee. There was a cell phone store where the man at the register had on his head a base-ball cap advertising a Formula 1 event in the 1990s. In the halal meat shop next door a queue of men just stood there waiting their turn to buy live chickens for slaughter for the purpose of dinner with the wife and children. When I turned around I made eye contact with a man in a long striped shirt who smiled and said to me: "Hello, baby." And I knew he could not be the boyfriend, so I continued onward, in silence, to the train and then I went deep into the underground where inside I saw a man with no shoes, his ankles bloated and covered in blood. He sat on a cardboard box and asked me if I had any money for him. I did not have money for him. It was a game-time decision, but I would not be giving him any of the various international currencies that sat there in my coin purse. I shut my eyes, hard. I swiped my MetroCard. The stairs were steep and, given that I was in espadrilles, there was a fear that maybe I'd trip and fall and the question of the boyfriend would become null because I'd be paralyzed; drooling into a paper cup, defecating into a plastic sack, convalescing in a hospital that I could never leave.

Here I was: Reality on the choo choo train. On this one the final stop was Jamaica–179th Street, but I'd be connecting to one where the direction was Forest Hills–71st Avenue. I sat down next to a man wearing Coke-bottle glasses. He was reading facts about the Vietnam War. When he flipped the page, he licked the tips of his fingers. The man had large thighs. He was in cargo pants. When the train swung through the tunnels I could hear the sound of keys and coins jiggling in his pockets.

Inside of my head I saw winning combinations on slot machines. A row of cherries. A row of limes. A row of chuckling boyfriends who, when you hit the jackpot, were singing your name out loud. The man with the glasses let out a burp. The train stopped and I knew instinctively through years of conditioning that this was where I was meant to get off. It was so hot underground. I was like a girl on a Venetian gondola piloted by a ghost. We all walked in a unified mass toward the next train. A woman selling mangoes asked me if I wanted some. There was a baby and it was screaming. I was concerned that my intuition was wrong. I swatted a fly away from my face. A rat scurried past me and I meditated on the idea that it was related to the one I'd seen die on the intersection that I'd be crossing in just a few minutes.

On the next train a man was saying curse words so loudly I had to cover my ears as protection so that it would not infect me. I was terrified of the swears puncturing my skull. It was just two stops now. Two: that was easy stuff. I squeezed my hand into a fist. I took a sip of my water. It seemed like it was full of guys in here. On the train, I mean. They were all looking at me. They were all speaking to me. They all gave me this look with their eyes where I could tell what they were saying in their heads was: *Reality. Sugar. Baby. Darling. Girl!!! We all love you here. The R train is Where It All Starts. Next Stop True Love. Next Stop Pretty Girl Gets a Kiss on the Lips.*

I couldn't stop smiling. It was like I was the pope in my little glass cage atop the big truck, waving at all the happy people down below.

When I got off the train, it was like saxophones were playing. The sky was a lovely shade of blue, and the clouds were of the white and puffy variety. On the street, cars honked their horns and I watched as they all came to a halt when the stoplight disintegrated into red. I took this as my sign that it was safe to cross. I kept my eyes peeled for any sign of rats. There were none. There was no carnage to behold. Instead, it was mostly businessmen carrying briefcases and ladies carrying cameras to make sure that everyone knew that vacation was fun. The mall stood there before me, glistening. Things were off to an auspicious start. I had begun my quest in earnest.

FOUR

The Atlantic Terminal Mall was one of my all-time favorite spots. It is a place wherein many of my happiest memories have occurred. For example, Soo-jin and I went once because Gwen asked her to buy a new printer. While Soo-jin chitchatted with a man named David about her options, I decided to have some fun. I went to the lowest level for a snack. It was the awning that piqued my interest: it advertised delicious chicken nuggets with seven different species of mustards. And it really was delicious. Just in case you were wondering.

This time I had a new reason to be here. I needed to find a boyfriend. I needed to do everything I could to secure him. I needed to make myself available.

Here is a fact about the Atlantic Terminal Mall: it is pretty big. You have to go down this escalator to go to the shops. The escalator is clear on both sides. For some, especially those suffering from vertigo, this is a cause for concern. It is le vide for them as opposed to the big heavens. For those of us who enjoy the exhilaration that comes with being on top of the world, it is a joyous occurrence.

As I stood there I surveyed my world. In front of me, men. Behind me, men. I was feeling a sense of mischief, so I didn't even hold on to the handrail. Above me I noticed that the ceiling was vaulted and this gave off the essence of the Catholic Church. Below me I heard children shouting about who stole a toy. There was also music playing. It was soft music. The artist was singing about true love. I wondered if he had

Atlantic Terminal Mall
"America's Heartland!"

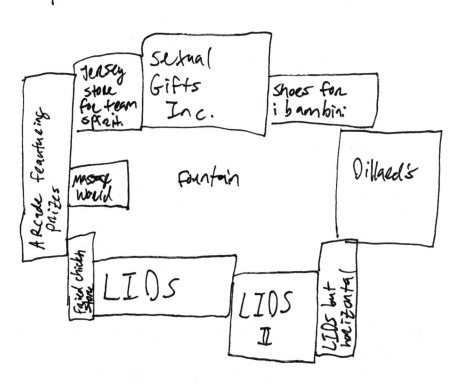

Jersey store for team spirit.

Sexual Gifts Inc.

Shoes for i bambini

Arcade Featuring Prizes

Massage World

Fountain

Dillard's

Fried chicken store

LIDS

LIDS II

LIDS but horizontal

ever been in a situation like the one I was in, where you wake up in your apartment and feel so keenly aware of your destiny.

Where was I to go now that I was here? If I were a boyfriend, where would I be? I seriously did not want to go to Lids, after what happened last time with Emil. Cross that off the list. Note to self: he's not in Lids. Maybe that meant this future boyfriend would be in a place where you can buy forty-five hot dogs featuring beef sauce. Or a video game arcade where winners receive prizes in the form of a green stuffed monkey with a perverted and questionable grin. No no. Not in there. Memory exercise time. I pulled a piece of paper out of my bag and quickly drew a map of the mall.

Something seemed off about the map. Sometimes the iron trap of Reality's mind produces a falsehood. I imagined that ne'er-do-wells were up there tinkering in the Gray Matter, creating beguiling fabulisms. Whatever. It was accurate, I think? I had to get serious. I guess I could get started at the emporium where you could buy various jerseys for sports teams? A boyfriend could be a footballer. Or the sexual store where they sold novelty bongs and devices? Thereby proving to me immediately of his skill when it came to amorous relations. Of course, there was also the children's shoe store. He could be in there. Maybe he was a babysitter. I wasn't sure I could accept a boyfriend who worked as a babysitter. It was smarter to look for a salaryman. A moneyed guy. The kind of man who has bank accounts in different states and countries. You know: he is rich. He will give Reality la vie oh so charmed. It's not so much that he can buy you items, it is that he is a Provider.

I decided to consult my copy of *Girlfriend Weekly* for further guidance:

HOW TO FIND THE MAN OF YOUR
DREAMS IN UNEXPECTED PLACES

For the discerning lady, to find the perfect man it is all about attitude. Bring a little charm with you everywhere that you go. For example, when you are at the grocer's, be sure to give a smile and a wink to the dashing gentleman in the porkpie hat. Say: "Gee whiz, woo-woo, you are a beautiful specimen and I am a virgin." Meanwhile, at bridge club, please remember to ask your girlfriends if there is a lucky fella who is looking for a young lady such as yourself. And remember, it is not considered crass to go steady with the divorced or widowed.

I pressed my palms to my temples. This was excellent advice, but I had to think harder. I wasn't about to take up bridge. He had to be somewhere.

Patience is very important in regard to the heart's quest. Rushing would lead to limited results. Oh, but I wanted him to appear soon! I wanted it to be easier than this. It was already so hard, putting oneself out there in this way. This was New York City. I was meant to be up in some art deco salon where the ceilings are gilded, and I am on a couch in the nude and the lighting is a mix of emerald and gold and the potted ferns are Brobdingnagian. There would be the telling of pleasantries in this room, such as this one from the times of ancient Sumer: A dog walks into a bar and says, *I cannot see a thing. I shall open this one.*

I decided to go to the fountain in the middle of the mall so I could become contemplative. I'd hold watch in the aquamarine waters of the fountain. I'd wait as the light slowly faded from blue to mauve to green and then black. In time I'd certainly see at least a few contestants and candidates. And plus, I was weary from my travails. I knew from my lessons of life that to attract a mate a good idea is to be passive. To let life leak in and out of you like chemicals in a pirouette dropper.

I took a penny from my rucksack and dropped it into the fountain. *Make a wish, Reality!* That was easy. I bet you can guess what I wished for. A boyfriend! I took a seat on the fountain's edge and surveyed the scene. This was a court for an esteemed girlfriend. Everyone here was now one of my subjects. I gave them all names. All of my subjects were now called Reality's Kids. They were my serfs. And when I became a girlfriend, my boyfriend would praise me for my ample dowry. "Nice dowry," he would say. "And what an interesting plot of land, the Atlantic Terminal Mall. These grounds are certainly not fallow."

I turned my head and noticed there was a man right there, next to me. This man was older, perhaps around fifty-seven. Meaning he was chock-full of wisdom, and also a bit bald, jaundiced, and he had some paunch around his stomach. He was wearing a pair of gray terry cloth sweatpants and a special T-shirt depicting a popular comic book character micturating on an image of the Red Sox baseball team logo. "Fuck Sox," said the shirt. Interesting choice. Very explicit but also states an opinion. The man was frankly an aesthete. I was interested. He was muttering to himself and also scratching his scalp, thereby creating a little white pile of dandruff that gave off the vibe of snow from heaven. But what was he saying? That's when I noticed he had steely blue eyes. Oh yes. This was certainly a playboy of the Western world. I bet he always was wooing ladies with his fabulous blue eyes and scalp-scratching technique. It was at this moment that I realized that there were hardly any people around. Now it was just me and this marvelous gentleman. How was I going to convince him that I was more than willing to go for a beverage of his choosing?

He began to rub his cock from inside his gray terry cloth sweatpants. Did no one else see him? He looked at me. His eyes were becoming very crazy, like the eyes that I associated with the wild dogs of my past. His muttering grew louder. "Bitch," he said in a honeyed baritone. "Come on. I know you like it when I touch it. I seen you around the baseball cap store." I mean, I did find the situation erotic, but this was not exactly boyfriend material. And I did enjoy a nice chapeau. Yet: this was not a man who would be proud of me for having a dowry of serfs called Reality's Kids. This was not a man who would agree that the Atlantic Terminal Mall had grounds that were certainly not fallow. No. I was done with this. This was the era of boyfriends. Opulent boyfriends. I had to get serious and here I was, getting distracted as all sin.

A great pain shot through my head. I had to get out of here. Even though I loved the mall I had a feeling that the only men who hung out here during the daytime were gentlemen like this one. Sexy, yet possibly someone with terrible intentions. Golly Goodness. Why had I trusted Emil? Even a wise man can be led astray in the kingdom of God, I suppose.

I pulled out my cell phone and called him. Just because I thought he ought to know that his advice wasn't really all that useful. He picked up after three rings.

"Emil," I said. "I could not find a boyfriend at the mall! My best option was a man touching his cock in front of a beautiful fountain."

"Reality," said Emil. "You need to stop calling me about what you do with other guys."

"Emil, if you will recall," I responded, "you've taken an interest in me finding a boyfriend. You went as far as to suggest that I check out the mall for this purpose. It was a terrible idea by the way. Especially after the Lids incident."

"Yeah but, like," said Emil, "that's on you. If you want a boyfriend you can't make me find you one. You can't make it my problem. Also, you have to for serious get over that thing at the Lids store. I got you a free hat."

"I see what you mean, Emil," I said. "And I do appreciate the free hat."

I could feel tears welling up in my tear ducts.

"Reality, are you crying?"

"No."

Streams fit for freshwater trout began to burst from my eyes.

"Eughahaa!" I said.

"Come on, girl. Stop. That's literally so manipulative."

FIVE

The party was in Gowanus. These were Emil's friends from college. When we walked over from the train he reminded me to "not tell people that we're sleeping together," because "guys looking for a girlfriend don't need to hear about some dude you're railing." I told Emil that his secret was safe with me and then we walked into a store that sold both fried chicken and Thai food because we needed to pick up a pizza for some reason. The store was very beautiful. My favorite part was that there was a piece of glass between us and the man who stood at the cash register. Emil placed the order and then we stood outside and smoked some cigarettes.

A man walked past us. He had long brown hair and looked a bit like a sad dog. "Yo! That's my friend Ariel," said Emil. "What's up, man. This is my cousin's half sister."

"Yo, dude," said the sad-eyed man named Ariel, shaking hands with Emil. "I actually gotta jet. See you in a few."

"No prob, boss, see you up there."

"Ok, bye," said Ariel. "Nice cousin." He looked at me and I looked at him, and then he hobbled away with a curious gait.

The pizza arrived. We went around the corner and walked up about two dozen stairs. The party was in a room with white floors and pink lights and a disco ball. It was bodies dressed in nighttime fineries which were smoking indoors. There was this communal bottle of gin featuring lime that everyone was drinking. On the stage a band played and it was all guitars and they were very loud. Emil disappeared into the fold. "I have to go talk to someone," was what he told me. As for me, well, now I was Reality—alone.

It was time to observe. Girlfriends were everywhere. I took notes. They wore velvet frocks, blouses covered in pieces of celestial glitter. They were whispering among each other. I wanted to be just like them. I wanted to be We. I wanted to be We Are Going on Vacation. I wanted to speak their secret language. I wanted a fine bottle of vino, ice cream, holding hands—they had this and I did not. The girlfriends were with their boyfriends. Their boyfriends had their arms around their waists. Their boyfriends were tired. Their boyfriends hoped it would be ok if they ducked out early because they needed to go home and sleep because they had a big day at work.

The boyfriends liked listening to the punk rock which was playing but what they really wanted to do was slowly drink a beer on the couch.

All of this was really magical to me. I was doing a great job in this environment. I was flirting. There were many possible candidates here at the DIY venue. I impressed all of them with my cacophonous laughter and convivial mood. I took sips of the communal gin because they did not serve vodka with egg. These were the kind of guys *Girlfriend Weekly* spoke of. These were New York City Cosmopolitans. They were urbane. They had boyish charm and searing intellects. None of them had expressed serious interest in me but it was fine. It was fine. I was not a failure because none of them had expressed serious interest in me yet.

I excused myself to the bathroom. "I am going to relieve myself," is what I said. I wasn't talking to anyone, it was more like a general announcement. I wanted to maintain an aura of politesse in case any of these floppy-haired boys in mechanic jumpsuits wanted to ask me to dance.

I twirled my dress and walked into the little bathroom. It had walls painted black as the night. I was Reality, danseuse, acrobat, girl-about-town in la dooooubla vay say (WC). I felt the bass in my hands as I pressed them to the toilet. I bent over so I could touch my toes. I suppose you could say that I was extremely drunk. It happens. Sometimes a would-be girlfriend gets a tad bit carried away. My eyes were seeing everything in a tunnel. A naked red bulb hung from the ceiling, making it seem like I was a leopard gecko in a cage. I grabbed my ankles and began to sway. I could stay like this forever. There was a future where instead of going back out to dance I could stay here forever and eat paper towels. I could drink the sink water. I had everything I could ever want in this room! It was way nicer than my apartment! I let out a ha ha ha.

I was doing so great! I was having an amazing time. It was growing unclear to me how long I had been here for. Was I a failure for not having immediately wowed one of these hommes? I was beginning to feel like a failure. It should be instantaneous. I needed to leave. I pulled on the doorknob but it would not turn. It would be just my luck that I would be trapped. I guess I was going to die here. I yelled. I beat my fists on the door. I yanked at the knob. I slammed the whole of my weight into its hinges.

A voice. I heard a voice.

"Open the door," it said.

"I am refreshing myself!" I responded. "I was just yelling and body-slamming the door to promote the punk rock spirit."

I heard a cymbal crash. I heard a drum fill. There was some more bass. Somewhere in the mix I could make out fragments of a singer, but I could not tell what he was singing.

"Are you on cocaine? Are you locked in there?" said the voice again. "You're Emil's cousin's half sister, right?"

It was Ariel! We had a real McCoy on our hands, this I believed to be true. The voice I heard was a guy who was both suave and street-smart—vetted nonetheless by one of the most esteemed people I knew. He was showing an interest. After all, he was the rescue committee. You didn't save someone from a locked bathroom stall if you think maybe that you do not want to give love a shot.

I gained my composure and strategized. As I saw it, I had two options:

1. I could stay in the bathroom until the fire department arrived and then maybe a firefighter would be my boyfriend.
2. I could let this Ariel rescue me and he could be my true love.

I flushed the toilet. I inspected my pupils in the mirror and was pleased to see they were normal. I looked at my dress and saw that it was neatly ironed. I smelled my underarms and the smell was baby powder. I looked at my eyes and they looked actually a bit glassy but otherwise I looked happy, healthy, and ready for hugs and kisses. The moments before he broke in were some of the longest in my life. I watched my surroundings flicker like Rorschach tests showing up on an old projector. I suddenly felt like I was inhabiting the whole of my body in an extreme, almost cannibalistic way.

I looked again at the wall. In white letters it said: PARADISE.

IN WHICH REALITY BRAVELY WORKS FOR

THE AFFECTION AND UNDYING LOVE OF THE

BOYFRIEND WHO WE NOW KNOW IS NAMED ARIEL

SIX

I now had an apple of my eyeball. And it was here, in Paradise (#221), where I lived with him—my true love. He spoke to me in the dulcet tones of the surfer Miki Dora. This is Ariel we are talking about—the rescue committee. Last name Koffman. Originally from the Greater Boston Area, but to me he sounded like he came from Malibu, California. Bornth in 1993 under the green ray of autumn. Under the sign of Sagittarius. A former child genius of the piano. A current doctoral candidate in the history of Mesopotamia, specializing in the Assyrian Empire.

He was Ariel Ariel Ariel. Koffman Koffman Koffman. And I was first name: Reality, last name: Kahn.

Ariel had long brown hair and big lips and the hazel eyes of an introspective family pet. He wore baggy shirts and pants that you wear if you are at prep school and shoes that you own if you are homeless. The main things we talked about were rock 'n' roll bands and the people and places we had seen and been before we met, before he busted down the door of the bathroom and I asked him if he would be mine. He was phunking with my heart.

I had since learned that Paradise was a DIY venue with a jazz twist. Me and Ariel were spending all of our days together there. Along with his roommates. There were several boys who lived there, in bedrooms that were shipping containers. They were all twenty-six and they met in a class where you read James Joyce and say your opinions. The Joycean Boys. The name Paradise came from Milton, which they had all read in the class and found to be very inspiring.

Here is how the first three months went: There were bowling alleys where we'd drink pitchers of cheap beer and bowl spares and what would happen is we'd get a little drunk and he'd grab my waist as we watched the ball knock down the pins. On some days we went to see rock 'n' roll in bombed-out basements where the toilets would not flush and others we'd eat salami-and-cheese sandwiches in gardens, and everyone was so nice and it was true that we looked so good.

It was the best when we sat around and did nothing. Do you know what I am speaking of? Like, you wake up at three in the afternoon after a night of smashing your parts together and then for breakfast it's waffles from the deli. And then you just keep rolling around like that. The light pools onto your skin and you look so very beautiful. You get all cross-eyed. You close your eyes and it is visions of mansard roofs and Bedouin tents. Strange marks appear on your neck, chest, ass. Maybe even a song plays and it's Cat Stevens singing about how la-la-la-la-la-la-la-la, la la it's a wild world and that you're like a child, girl. And then if your name is Ariel Koffman this is the part where you point to Reality and say: "That's you!"

Here's another thing we'd do: sit on the roof and read books and drink beers and when we finished them we would throw them off the roof and watch as they splattered into millions of little crystalline shards. We called it bottle drop and you won if you didn't hit anyone on the head or something.

In those primordial days I weighed three pounds and the rest was just air. When I went home to Soo-jin and Lord Byron they remarked that I seemed happier and I believed that my cheeks had turned a beautiful shade of coral red. Emil and I saw each other less and were no longer having intercourse, but when I did go buy drugs, he'd give me a warm hug and say: "Girl, you deserve this. Koffman's a chill guy," and "I guess I can't hit that anymore." I could tell he was proud of me for finally having a suitable hobby.

And then it became every day. I went home less often. A pile of my panties got starchy and smelly in a corner. I became a fixture in Paradise.

Would you blame me? I had never done romance before. And here he was: strong, beautiful Ariel who was all for me.

It was now early summer; it was a bottle-drop day. We were drinking our beers and watching them fall. Ariel was reading a book about the history of the Assyrians, and I was reading a romance novel where two horses fall in love a very long time ago:

> Miss Sunshine wasn't like any of the other horses. She was different. When she trotted you could see every muscle in her body flex. It was like magic. It was like God himself was helping her glide across the farmlands. That's what Brown Bartholomew loved most about her: how natural she made it all look. Pure ecstasy. His horse cock was rock hard just thinking about it. What wonders lay inside of her? In her warmest regions?

"She is a very good horse," I said in a whisper. "This will be the one for Brown Bartholomew. This much is certain."

"What?" responded Ariel.

"I am speaking of what I am reading right now," I said. "It is a tale of a horse who is looking for love. His name is Brown Bartholomew and the apple of his eye is named Miss Sunshine."

"Is that like a book you bought at the supermarket?" said Ariel.

"At supermarkets you can buy many useful items," I responded.

A cool wind blew through my hair. I looked up and the clouds were a streak of pillowy white. And there were birds, too. Rats of the sky. I wondered if pigeons ever got crushed by a lowrider Fiat car. They were singing and telling each other stories. I assumed they were letting each other know where the tastiest garbage was.

It was a warm day. One of those days where spring melts delicately into summer and the children outside are in short pants and when you take a sip of a soda pop it does not feel like an assault on your internal body temperature. Down below there were teenagers on skateboards and entire families gathered around speakers listening to music about kissing as they waited patiently for the hot dogs and hamburgers to cook. I stood up and looked across: on the roofs of our neighbors there were fine linens, swaying in the breeze. The neighbors were all sitting out on plastic folding chairs in red and white and yellow, and I believe I glimpsed at least one naked pair of breasts. There was more music: a click track, a shuffling drum machine, synthesizers that came from 1982, female voices that sounded as if they were pumped with helium.

I looked again at Ariel.

"Ariel," I asked him, taking my hands and brushing the pleats on my tennis skirt.

"Hnnnnfg??" responded my darling.

"Are you my boyfriend now? I assume this is so, but we have not discussed it."

"This guy I know just texted me and said he has these Serbian research chemicals he got on the dark web," said Ariel.

"Ariel, I am very interested in these chemicals, but you did not respond to my question," I said, gazing at my feet.

"We're having fun! We're hanging out! It's been three months. Are you horny? I'm kind of horny."

"Yes it has been three months, and that is why I am confirming the question of boyfriend," I said, raising one of my eyebrows with expert precision. Additionally it was correct to say that I was in an amorous mood.

"It's nice when you do that thing with your eyebrow."

And then he walked over to me and we began to do kissing. His tongue was a warm pulse inside my mouth. It was like a snake poking around in there. A black mamba. A rattler. A viper. I began to feel very sticky. I think this was because of the heat. It was the blue of noon, which meant that it was the hottest it would be all day. I was also perhaps sticky because it seemed I was growing hot for Ariel. We were in noli me tangere mode right now but that would end momentarily.

Ariel and I had done sex many times at this point. We had done this in the sink and in the bed and on the couch and in all the shipping container bedrooms and on the roof and on a wrought-iron bench on the glittering black waters of the Gowanus. We had done it backward and forward and to the side, and on one memorable occasion, while watching a television show where a lady sells you bracelets for a low price of $19.99 (this instance was at the Talia Laundromat on Bond and Sackett).

Ariel was very athletic in the art of the sexual, and I was seriously amazing at knob slobbing. It was a real gift. And I was so lucky to have this because a girlfriend must be able to suck cock. I had learned it from a man who we will call the European; me and the European met while I was summering in the Slovakian countryside and was in some need of jam and cheese from the local market and he, too, had the same objective. It was a summer romance. Goldenrods, thyme, Cinzano in a pale green cup with a single ice cube. A paisley couch on a back porch. It was every day, mostly in the afternoon, that he sat me down and said: "Please, no teeth! You are making it hurt very badly." And I learned, oh how I learned. I went up and down. I whispered to the shaft so it would do what I pleased. The European would convulse and I would feel him begin to drip inside of my mouth and the foreign sentences he uttered were those of immense pleasure.

And then it was the 11:30 a.m. plane out of Bratislava. And then the present transitioned to memory and the European became a dream on my cell phone. I still heard from him. It was quarterly. He would often send me a website link to a video of a svelte Cuban man singing the songs not of love but of pure, carnal ecstasy. And I would always respond: "Thank you, the European!" This was one of my best sexual memories.

Ariel did not know these facts about me. He was not under the impression that I was virginal Reality, but I was shrouded in mystery for him. This was nice for me because I felt confident that to be a girl-friend, an amazing thing to do is have your past be a void.

A void! A void! I was avoiding Ariel's gaze as he laid me out on the twin cot which had no sheets or pillows, in the street-facing shipping container where the window was the size of a thimble and outside the room what I heard was the sound of two guitars yelling at each other over hills and valleys of fuzz and delay.

What were the names of the United States presidents? In alphabetical order. It goes Adams, John; Adams, John Quincy. I felt Ariel thrust himself into my organ. *What will I eat for dinner later?* I felt the warmth of his breath hovering on the crook of my neck. *The Assyrians were a decadent and licentious culture, this is what you must know.* I shut my eyes.

Here are the facts: I left my body and there I stood, a glowing orb named Reality. She was of the same constitution as the Oracle of Delphi. She was fey and fecund. She was wearing a very beautiful dress of white organdy with blue and green and purple flowers. They brushed out her hair and put it into braids. They had her lie out in a coffin made of glass. On the base of the coffin there was a soft, downy layer of bluish-green grass. And then once she was settled they dropped the coffin into the river and they had her float just like so until she reached the sandy shores of a place which was rumored to be called Mount Nothing.

I realized that my sweet darling Ariel was ejaculating inside of me and I walked right out of the door of my mind and, like a child who has almost drowned and who now gasps for air on the coast of safety, I came, too.

SEVEN

There was a train and then there was a bus and now we were walking up
a staircase where the walls were painted yellow and they were chipped
and the stairs were hard and metal and were a pea green color. Ariel was
very excited about his Serbian chemicals, whose purpose was a mystery
to me. I was just happy to be there. Any time with my sweetheart, Ariel,
was considered fortuitous. I did wonder if these Serbs were good or
bad. I made a note to ask them if they were all benevolent forces on
this cruel planet.

It was one flight then two flights and then we were climbing the
ranks to vast celestial zones. The apartment building had no elevator.
I huffed and puffed like I was some kind of sherpa of the hills. Finally
we arrived at the door. A dog with a deep, meaty bark began to growl. I
looked above me and I noticed there was a dirty skylight, and next to
it, a single hanging bulb where a colony of flies buzzed in concentric
circles. It was like they were doing a rain dance, which is what you do if
you want to maaaake it raiiiiin.

"One minute," said a voice. It was accented. It was a foreign voice.

I heard the sound of someone fumbling with the latch, and then
the door swung open. On the other side was a man who was short and
had a marvelous, shiny head. Next to him, a dog with gray fur. I believe
that the genre of this dog was that of the pit bull breed.

"You are here to see about some chemicals?" he whispered.

"Yeah, man, thanks for hooking it up," said Ariel.

"Ok, well, if you would enter now I will show these to you," said
the man.

"It is a beautiful dog that you have," I interjected. "It is a fine dog, and I admire its coat. Gray is a magnificent color for this fido of yours."

The man blinked at me and said: "Her name is Urszula."

And I said: "I will never forget the beautiful dog known as Urszula."

"Is she of, ah, how do you say in English? Very idiotic? She has been kicked in the head by a horse?" he asked Ariel.

"Nah, man, she's just like that," he responded.

The apartment smelled of fried food mixed with pine-scented air freshener. I was instructed to sit down while Ariel and the guy went to the other room for the chemicals. A TV was switched on, and on it they were advertising an amazing new type of medicine that if you are a man and sometimes it is hard for you to perform sexually inside of a woman's organ, you can get some assistance. I was very transfixed. A man was climbing a mountain with a beautiful lady, taking in the vistas.

"Thanks to Adonis-XR, me and my wife, Rebecca, can climb the Matterhorn every night!" he said.

Then the name of the drug flashed on the screen in a beautiful cursive font, alongside the name of Dr. Zweig Altmann and some facts about how a possible side effect was that you might want to kill yourself.

This did not seem like medicine that Ariel needed. He was always ready to go in sexual matters. This was one of the many things that I enjoyed about Ariel. He was a real go-getter. He had a zest for life. He was always saying stuff like "I want to cream inside of you" and "Take your fingers and put them in your pussy and tell me how wet I make you." Me and Ariel, we loved intellectual conversations such as these ones. I was so lucky that I had such a special guy to chitchat with all the time.

And then, just like that, I remembered the conversation from earlier. I played it back in my head. I could smell Ariel. I could feel the wind on my skin. It was like the burning of a cyanotype.

Boyfriend . . . He does not want to be My Boyfriend! screamed my brain.

I envisioned myself falling off a cliff of Sounion and into the sea just like King Aegeus. What was I to Ariel? Was I simply an organ in which to engage in intercourse? Was I just supposed to sit pretty in saddle shoes with a communist reader in my lap? Was I a wide-eyed girl he had picked to hear his theories about the Assyrians? It was true that he was an excellent scholar, and I felt confident he would have much success in this field.

It was not clear to me what purpose I served Ariel. As for me, it was obvious. Ariel was the boyfriend. He was going to imbue my life with meaning! I was an outline on the page, and he was going to color me in! Oh, my sweet Ariel. I really did hope that he was going to take me to destinations both international and physiological just like in *Girlfriend Weekly*. I envisioned trips to the pyramids of Egypt via an ancient Concorde airplane as well as luncheons at esteemed picnic tables in port cities and long, winding discussions about the nature of art. I needed to pay attention to this. I needed to remember the possibilities of love. L. O. V. E. Ariel, he would see in due time that this love was true and that our boyfriend-girlfriend destiny was a factual thing.

I noticed the TV was now playing a commercial where a lawyer tells you how to get money for various workplace injuries. It was starring a woman wearing a construction hat who reveals she has gotten a boo-boo from a bulldozer and thanks to the lawyer who goes by the name of Mazotti Esq., she is now flushed with funds.

I now felt calm. It was nice to see there were people out there who change lives. I loved the TV. I love television. It was from a young age that I loved television. I could sit there for hours. I was on a little island. I almost forgot where I was but then I looked at the floor and I remembered that in the house of Soo-jin, Lord Byron, and Reality, the floors were not parquet and the walls were not painted the color of red wine and we did not have signs bornth of wood that said: "Live Laugh Love."

And at home we did not have all of these Serbs walking about. This was something I had just noticed. I had been so absorbed by the television and my love for the moving image that I did not realize that along with the owner of the beautiful dog called Urszula, there were between five and seven other men who were walking around and speaking to each other in a dialect I could not quite understand. I assumed they were talking about how there was currently a beautiful girl who is sitting on the ground watching commercials. Perhaps they were speaking of the items to buy at the store. Or maybe it was political matters or they were whispering about the chemicals from Serbia. I thought about telling one of them that I had spent significant time on the Continent, that I was versed in the fall of Yugoslavia, that I even knew a useful expression in the Serbo-Croatian language, mineralna voda, but then decided it would be rude to disturb the flow of conversation, so I just sat there in front of the television awaiting further instruction.

Some more minutes passed and then Ariel and the owner of Urszula rematerialized in the television chambers. They were speaking softly to each other and I watched as Ariel exchanged a wad of dollar bills for a paper bag coated in grease. The two men shook hands. I always like to watch men touch palms. It is a very gorgeous thing to witness. They were walking toward me. I was happy to see my baby safely returned to me. I liked to know where Ariel was at all times. A part of me thought, *If I cannot see him, then it is likely he is dead, perhaps by the hands of another man or He has been killed by a Bear which lurks in the park. There are several of these in New York City and They Are Not Documented by Law Enforcement Because Moral Panic Would Surely Ensue.*

I blinked my eyes three times after this thought skirted through my brain. And then I noticed Ariel's gaze was fixed upon my face. Oh! What a beautiful visage did the man have. Oh! What a beautiful visage with the wet pebble of a freckle in the eyelid and where the hair and eyes are this shock of brune that did delight the heart. I was addicted to this body he inhabited. This sinewy body, which to me was like the feather on the willow tree. I wanted to kiss it but restrained myself because it was not in my nature to scandalize the Serbs. I had to maintain the current level of repartee. I had to maintain my positionality as some kind of chatoyant sex crystal.

I saw words form in his eyes. And then I heard the words bubble out of his mouth.

"Ok, Reality, ready to go?" said Ariel.

"Yes, I am ready to leave, Ariel. Have you accrued the Serbian research chemicals? Did you want to go dutch on them? That means to split in half," I responded.

"Jesus, Reality," said sweetie pie baby. "Can you say that, like, any louder?"

I could feel myself begin to get emotional again. I could not allow myself to make such a great error and I thought that I deserved to be tased with a taser.

"Please forgive me, Ariel," I responded.

Ariel brushed his beautiful wavy brown hair out of his eyes and clutched the paper bag closer to his chest.

"Reality . . ." he said. And then we were out the door. And then we were walking down the stairs and into the street, which smelled so much like freezer-burned meats and Mexican beer. As we inched closer and closer to the subway, I realized that what I was doing was digging my nail into my palm and when I inspected it I became violently aware that my hand was leaking bright red. I said nothing. I did nothing. I just continued to walk in a straight line and then we boarded the train and there was no fanfare and no one blew us kisses.

We just slumped into the orange-and-red subway benches and Ariel put his head on my shoulder and I put my hand on his leg and he fed me the chemicals and around me everything got hazy and then quiet and the colors grew brighter but also softer and I became the creature of Mount Shasta and I shouted of wanting to forage and dig and crawl inside of my volcano. When we walked from the train, Ariel pointed a flashlight at a brick wall and we solved the maze and I really really really really was so in love with him and it really really really felt like I had found my purpose and therefore was enlightened so I told him this and he kissed me on the nose and reminded me that I was high and suddenly it started raining and when I fell on the ground there were tears in my eyes and at the front door of Paradise he carried me in his arms and up and up and up we went, toward heaven.

EIGHT

I did not want to leave Paradise that morning but Ariel insisted that he needed to be out of the house and that I couldn't stay because if I needed to go to the store to buy a tampon or something else for my pussy, there might not be anyone to let me back in. I thought about arguing with him, of telling him that I would be happy to sit in his room all day like a captain's wife waiting on a wharf, but then decided if I did this it might prevent him from making the decision that we were boyfriend-girlfriend. And this was paramount. I needed to do everything I could to make this happen.

And I understood that Ariel was conducting important research that would take him all the way to the annals of New York University, but if I could not stay in Paradise, perhaps he could find some way to include me in these plans. Oh? He is off to go teach some eighteen-year-olds with strange blue hair from Newton, Massachusetts, and Bethesda, Maryland, about Antiquity in the Fertile Crescent? Reality can sit in the back very silently in a cloak so as not to disturb the learning processes. Reality can sit there, entombed in all black, reading religious texts. *I know what the Talmud is! I have heard of the temples of Bacchus and Augustus!* I wanted to shout to Ariel as he grabbed his backpack and stuffed it with various loose pieces of paper as well as the computer. *I, too, am well-versed in ancient ways of seeing and knowing!* I wanted to say, even though this was a falsehood.

But I said none of this at all. I waved adieu to my dearest and then I thought about what I could possibly do without the presence of Ariel. I supposed it could make sense for me to do a commercial. I did need money. My meals were not all paid for. What would I do if suddenly I had to buy new panties? Also, I needed to contribute to Soo-jin, Lord Byron, and Reality's home, even though I was so rarely ever there. Another thing is that girlfriends must busy themselves and a job is a good way to do this.

I pulled out my cell phone and dialed up the number of Jethro, who was my agent. If you will remember, I am an actress for water park commercials. This is my only profession. Ok but anywho, Jethro was responsible for my three water park commercials. I met Jethro because I was sitting pretty at the bikini store and trying on the latest styles. Meanwhile, Jethro was lurking in the changing area, in search of the latest talent. I remember what he said when he saw me: "You have that real Hollywood lady charm, little miss." And I remember saying: "The bathing suit is a conduit to a good time."

So when I called, Jethro picked up on the first ring.

"Reality, my special lady, how's it going, we haven't heard from you in a while. We want to make you a star," said Jethro.

"Hello, Jethro," I responded in an assertive tone of voice. "As you will know I do the water park commercials for my income."

"I've seen you on those twisty loop-de-loop slides. No other actress in the Northeast has your technique and command," he said.

"So tell me this: Do you have a commercial for me?"

"Well," said Jethro. "Times have been tough. They sure have. You'll understand. The economy etcetera etcetera. But here's the thing. Paramus, New Jersey. There's a new park going up, and we need a girl who is fearless and comfortable with wearing a high-cut bikini. I think you just might be the girl. What do you say? Have you shaved your pussy recently?"

What an amazing coincidence that when I called Jethro he would have work for me that very day! I had not shaved my pussy but that could be rectified. I mused on this notion of the waterslides and Paramus and the high-cut bikini, and then I saw the face of Ariel. It was as if his face were fixed upon the sun. When the sun shined, you saw Ariel.

Similar to the television baby sun from the past. *Will Ariel be proud if I do the Paramus job?* I wondered. It was essential that while Ariel spoke of the earliest written laws and the story of an eye for an eye that I, too, left my mark on the world. And goddamn, I was great at my job. And, of course, there was the problem that funds were dripping out fast. The cash was leaking out of my eyeballs.

"Jethro," I said. "I will do the water park commercial. I will come to Paramus."

I heard Jethro breathe into his cell phone. It was a hot breath. It was a labored breath.

"Alright, Reality, we'll see you on set in three hours. I'll send a car."

It was a lap of luxury on the ride over to the water park. Jethro was a fan of lavishing me, as I had that Hollywood thing, and he was certain I'd be a star. As for me, I did not want the fame and the fortune. I wanted to be a girlfriend. I wanted to be boyfriend and girlfriend with Ariel. The lights, the fans, this did not appeal to me, but I knew I was good at going down those slides, so for Jethro, I'd be the waterslide queen, if only for the afternoon.

The car was black and when I stepped inside it smelled of cinnamon and burnt leaves and the driver, an older man, a man of perhaps seventy or eighty years of age, offered me some mints. I said no thank you, I'm not in a mint mood. And he nodded his head and began to play the oh so sweet and sad music of lands so far away. Violins, accordions. A voice that shuddered with sadness. And outside the windows I watched as the streets I walked on with Ariel disappeared out of view.

Ariel.
Where was he?
Ariel.

He is meant to be.
With me!!!!!!!!!!!!!!!!!!

Would he know where I was? Would he be worried? I was concerned Ariel would think I was dead. I often thought he was dead when I did not know of his whereabouts.

Once again, I was making cell phone moves. I was making texting moves. It was the free jazz of Reality's mind. I was thinking of just what to say, and how. It was important to be smooth. I had to maintain an aura of nonchalance. I began to draft what to say in the prism of my thoughts:

Oh me? No, not such a busy day, oh but I am in a town car on my way to Paramus. Yeah. In New Jersey. It's not a big deal. No no no no. My agent, yes I have this, Jethro ... He has informed me that my destiny is to become a star. A celebrity in the making. I am bashful so I don't care for this. Yeah. Ok. Anyways, it's not a big deal but I'm going to do a commercial. I'm known for my fearlessness. I'm the queen of the slides. Don't know when I'll be back. You are my sweetie pie baby.

But no! I could not say this. Too much. Too much of too much.

So instead I wrote:

Hi, Ariel. It's Reality. I hope you are well. Anyways, I'm doing a water park commercial today in New Jersey. Do let me know if you will be ready to see me when I return.

Yours,
Reality

And hit send on my cell phone and then I turned it off and I said to the driver that I was ready for the mints. He pushed them out of the mint tube and I reached out my hand and slapped them into my mouth. I fished around in my rucksack for my sunglasses and put them onto my face as I sucked the spearmint from the sugared disks. I asked the driver to roll the windows down and he did this and the blare of the music dissipated out of the windows and changed textures. I knew from my years of study that this is called the Doppler Effect.

We pulled into a parking lot that was empty save for a few vans that I was sure were for the crew, and the orange Dodge Charger that on the license plate read the word *Jethro*. This, of course, was Jethro's whip.

I had been in Jethro's whip before because this is where he liked to have our very important meetings. Here is what we would talk about: me, my career, my potential, my rising star. I'd pose in my bikinis and he would graciously give me feedback. "It's about posture, chickadee," he'd say. "The way to sell the slide is to sell yourself, you have to give them that razzle-dazzle." It took me quite some time as well as instruction to learn that this did not mean twirling sparklers or a two-sided rapier. Eventually what I learned is that to be the best water park actress on the Eastern Seaboard it is about sweetness, about being a kind of demi-mondaine girl Friday with the largest smile and utmost confidence. It is about having poise. About being atop the slide and conveying to your audience that yes, you are fearless and fancy-free. And yet, it was short-lived, my etiquette lessons. There was something I was feeling that was not exactly razzle nor was it dazzle about Jethro's desire to have me pose in one of "those little cheerleader skirts." I struggled to figure out how this would contribute to my skill as an actress or to my general bonhomie.

Now I was in the Paramus Slippery Slide Wonderland parking lot hoping, praying, dreaming of becoming a girlfriend. I felt as if surely after Ariel received the news that my star was rising, he would drop all notions that we were "hanging out" and join me on the gilded escalator up to heaven where boyfriends and girlfriends kiss and wave at the people down below who are less lucky.

I smiled as I thought about this. I could sense that my luck would soon change. I knew that everything was about to go Reality's way. All I had to do was kill it on the slides, so I walked up to Jethro's whip and knocked on the window. He was in there. I could see him. And also, I could smell him. I could smell his strange and exotic cologne that he wore, the one I had seen him once purchase at a store where you can also obtain condoms, tampons, chocolate bars, greeting cards, and delicious cough medicine. It cracked open my brain, and I felt like I was beautiful cosmic Reality. I grinded my jaw. For a second, I thought I heard jazz again. A rat-a-tat on a drum kit, and then a Rhodes piano. Then, inside of my mind a familiar voice began to sing: *MOUNT NOTHING! ONE DAY THIS IS A PLACE WHERE YOU WILL GO!*

I snapped out of it. I seriously did not have time to figure out what any of that meant. Just as I was reorienting myself in the world of the Paramus Slippery Slide Wonderland, Jethro walked out of his Charger. He was wearing a cowboy hat, a powder blue suit and a pair of shiny black boots.

"Why hello there, Reality," said Jethro, flashing his beautiful white teeth. "It is a pleasure to have you back on set. Thank you for being available, especially at the last moment. The folks here at the Paramus Slippery Slide Wonderland sure are excited to meet you."

"Hi, Jethro. Thanks. And besides, nice cowboy hat," I responded.

"You got some spunk, little miss," said Jethro, taking in my form so as to be sure it was ready for the demands of the day's work. "Genuine Stetson, the hat that is. If you want, I can put you in touch with my guy. Guy in Midtown. Goes by the name of Mick, Mick Doyle. Irish guy. Mean as hell, alcoholic, that goes without saying, but he has great hats."

"Ok, Jethro," I responded again. "Thanks again, where is the hair and makeup area? I am assuming 'go time' is soon."

"Sure thing, let's get you ready for the slides," said Jethro, putting his hand around the small of my back. Once again I heard the familiar voice: *SOON IT WILL ALL MAKE SENSE NEXT YEAR IN MOUNT*

NOTHING! What was Mount Nothing? No. I really could not think about that right now! I was not some kind of Late-Stage Empire Shiksa. I was trying to be in Reality qua Reality mode?

So if you've never done a water park commercial before, here's the thing: they are so much fun, but also, they're a lot of work, which is why I have only done three of them and as a result am always scrambling for cold hard cash. But anyways. It's really about the glam. You get to sit in a chair and a lady who is named Linda, for example, calls you a pretty young thing and then asks if there's someone special. And for the last three times, when this Linda asked this, I would say, "No, but I love to fuck!" And this Linda would say, "Darling, you are a riot."

Today, the Linda in question was named Tina, and Tina was a Paramus native. She had pretty brown eyes and an apron with smiling girls and hearts. Using my detective skills, which I first developed at age six grâce à one missing periwinkle plastic shovel from the sandpit of life, I found out via Tina that she had twin sons named Raphael (nickname: Raffie) and Adrian (no nickname, although his grandmother sometimes calls him Addie, which drives him mad, absolutely mad). Tina's sons were in middle school, which was definitely hard but the boys were thriving as much as anyone can at that age. I could tell that Tina loved her boys and this made me smile even though I was not supposed to move my mouth as she applied the lip liner.

"Ok, honey," said Tina about a minute later. "I'm done with the lip liner."

"Does this mean I can smile again?" I asked Tina.

"Let's see those pearly whites shine," she said.

Without missing a single second, I let my pearly whites shine.

"You're a champ. You're making my day, you're such a hoot. And so sweet. And those teeth! You have a gorgeous smile," said Tina. "Tell me, do you have anyone special? Like a boyfriend?"

"I am so happy you have asked me this, Tina," I said. "I do, in fact, have someone special. His name is Ariel and he is perhaps about to be my boyfriend. Well. I mean to me he is my boyfriend, but he has not yet confirmed this, so things are a bit up in the air. And anyways, he has the voice of the surfer Miki Dora, and beautiful flowy brown hair and also he is doing graduate studies on the Assyrian Empire, which is how he makes money."

"Wow, that is so amazing!" said Tina. "A beautiful girl like you deserves such a handsome boyfriend who looks like a surfer named Miki Dora. Boyfriends are one of the most important parts of life! Ok, last thing: lip gloss!"

There is nothing more beautiful to me than a waterslide. There are many reasons for this. For one, a waterslide will take you places. You start up in the heavens, kissing the sky, you are an angel. Then there's gravity. The push and pull that keeps us here on Earth. As you get in position, it's already at work. It is already pushing you down, even before you know it. A waterslide is a journey. It is a head rush. When I am on a slide I think to myself: *Heaven could be this way.* And it is. It is such a beautiful thing to be flying through space and time and feeling the water on your body and for a brief instant knowing it could all go horribly wrong but also having this deep, intense faith in yourself to *Remain in Position at All Times.*

As I stood there on the top of the slide, which I'd been told is the Pirate's Plank Twisty Ride, I looked down below. It would be a steep drop. And I was doing a job. I was an actress. I was an actress up here in the paradise of the sky, awaiting her cues. I was in position. I was in hair and makeup. I had allowed them to wax my pubic hair off, so I now had the beautiful alopeciaed pubis of a seven-year-old. The bathing suit, of course, was a Jethro joint: he'd picked it out. I had let him. It certainly caused me to look like a disgusting slut, but once again, I was a professional. I was considered one of the best waterslide commercial actresses on the Eastern Seaboard. They spoke of me often in the community.

"Do you remember your lines?" asked Jethro. "We have cue cards, but you're such a pro I bet you have them memorized."

"Here at the Paramus Slippery Slide Wonderland," I said in a cheerful voice, "we love slides!"

"That's my girl. That's Reality," said Jethro, gesturing at me to the various crew members. "This woman, this girl, she's gonna put you all on the map. This here's a star in the making."

I bowed my head deeply. I was grateful for the praise.

"Alright, folks," said a man wearing a baseball cap with the name of a team from NYC. "Rolling, take one."

"Action. Action. Quiet on the set," said another.

I took a deep breath.

"Here at the Paramus Slippery Slide Wonderland, we love slides!" I said. "Follow me for more fun on rides such as the amazing Pirate's Plank Twisty Ride. Argh! Hear ye, hear ye. I am going to walk this here plank."

Like an opulent fish with metallic green gills, I made my way down the slide. It was magic. On the slide I felt the whole world opening up and expanding. Time became a whirlpool. Time was like one giant waterslide. The clouds felt as if they were moving, fast. The sun beat down on me and I could feel it kissing my flesh. I was so good at this. It felt so wonderful to feel this way.

It was so fleeting. I hit the pool, and I could see the cameras, and I felt like I needed just one more moment so I stayed there and I could see the bubbles rising and how glassy the world looked from down below me and as I surfaced and gasped for air, my mind's eye became inundated with the idea of Ariel again. I saw his hair and his eyes and I heard his laugh and I hoped he would be proud of me for my amazing work today but I was just not sure it would be enough. I was not sure that my incredible twists and turns on the Pirate's Plank Twisty Ride would convince him that I was just the girl to be his girlfriend whom he would bring to parties and say: "Hi! And this is my girlfriend, Reality!"

They gave me a towel and I dried off, thoroughly. Jethro came up to me to inform me that they got it all on the first take and that I was a star, a real star, a true professional, amazing on the slides. He then informed me that the check would be for a few grand and asked me if I was still living in that Kensington shitbox. I smiled and said I was.

My phone! my brain chirped.

Now that I was on dry land, I could see what Ariel had said to me about this accomplishment. I was so curious to see what he said! I bet he was so proud. I certainly hoped he would be.

I pulled my phone out of my rucksack and pressed a button to illuminate it.

I had no missed messages.

I clicked on Ariel's name and there it stood, my lonely lonely lonely message. Blinking out there in the world, signaling to no one nothing.

NINE

When I got back to Paradise all of the boys were sitting around. I counted them on my fingers and I saw that they were twelve today. Twelve boys from the James Joyce Opinions Class. I did not know any of their names, although I suspected that one of them was named Derek. And there was also Aziz but he wasn't really a Joycean Boy because he lived in his own apartment and had a profession that even came with health insurance. He was just there a lot because he was a genius of the drums. Ariel and the Joycean Boys. What did they do all day anyway? They were such special boys. Probably their main activities were playing around with their little pianos they bought on the website Craigslist and then bringing winsome females over for intercourse. I saw them milling about, these beautiful females.

"It's me, Reality!" I said to the room.

The Joycean Boys were playing their instruments with much patience and did not respond. I had heard a rumor that they were making some Afrobeat music after purchasing the appropriate synthesizers on the Craigslist web page. One of them, a dashing gentleman wearing a hat signifying a love for the baseball team Yankees, pulled out a marijuana joint and took a long drag. I think this was the one named Derek.

"Oh hey, Reality," he said. "Want some?"

I did. So I fixed my skirts and sat down. We were in the main room, which is where all the various instruments were. On the floor lay a beautiful rug with origins from Morocco. I believe it was a gift from one of the boys' parents. That was the thing about the boys: their mommies and daddies were always sending them stuff. It was usually aromatic spices (rosemary, thyme, saffron) and blankets (of soft cashmere and wool blends) and rugs (from Morocco or Santa Fe) and birthday cards (Dear One of the Joycean Boys, Happy twenty-sixth birthday!) and checks in amounts between two hundred and five hundred dollars (in one case, it was ten thousand dollars, from one of the members whose father was a banker, a salaryman, Mr. Moneybags), which they were always immediately cashing and then using the wonderful wonderful money to buy new pianos and guitars and then playing with them when they weren't busy finding new winsome ladies for intercourse.

The joint made its way to me and I pulled on it so I could do an awesome fire-breathing dragon move and watch it all pool out of my petite nostrils. I could tell that I was about to get a lot of help from this group of fast friends.

"Ok. So, boys, and by the way, I am wondering if you know where Ariel is. I have not heard from him all day despite the fact that I sent him a text informing him that I would be on set at a water park all day shooting a commercial, which is my profession."

"That's a job?" said one of the boys.

Good, we were on the right track! This jeune homme was asking some preliminary probing questions to help me on my journey to track down my darling boy so I could continue to be perfect for him.

"No texts from Ariel," said another, shaking a maraca. "It's not like he's dead or anything."

I waited for a moment. No one made any further inquiries into my plight.

This was a deplorable situation. Into Ariel's room I went. I suppose it was good that I was here first so I could welcome him home and give him a kiss on the cheek. But did he want me to do this? The boys were right, he was most likely still alive. He was probably on his way home. He was probably just on the subway. He was probably just eating a hot dog in front of one of those little carts. He probably just needed space! I remembered this is something boyfriends often like from girlfriends. They like space! They like for their lady to be neither seen nor heard. It reminded me of something I once read in *Girlfriend Weekly*:

SPACE: MAN'S "BFF"

Good evening from our Lisboa offices, ladies! If you are with your true love, you may have noticed that he is in need of space. This can be as simple as your true love getting on his horse and riding into town to pick up bread and jam at the local farm stand. It could also be by the waterways and aqueducts that he will travel. The blue Danube is considered a fan favorite among our guys. He will go on a canoe ride straight through the heart of Wien and will tell you about how the solitude, yes, the solitude, it is very good for the brain. As is a hike through the Julian Alps, with simply just his guide and of course he, too, will need a pack mule for the excursion. Our men need space. They must roam through these remote pastures of our fine continent in order to come up with inventions, treatises, and fine cuisines.

I was worried I couldn't give Ariel the space he needed. For a moment I considered maybe going back to the home of Reality, Soo-jin, and Lord Byron. But no! I could not do this. And besides, the boys loved me! They were so happy to see me. And I was happy to see them.

I could hear them playing their instruments right now! It was their new arpeggiator!

And it was an amazing sound that the arpeggiator made, but it was distracting me. Maybe there were clues in Ariel's room. I peeked underneath his bed and what I saw was empty containers of Thai food that me and Ariel purchased at the Thai place that also sells pizza. I looked on his desk and there were various academic texts that I was sure would not mean a thing to me as I knew I was nowhere nearly as smart as my sweetie. I licked my finger to turn the page of one book titled *The Assyrians: Their Culture, and Their Failures*, and began to read a chapter on the kinds of tunics they wore back then. It was fascinating, but it did not lead me closer to any truths regarding Ariel's whereabouts.

It was around this time that I began to strip. Something that I do is that I will often disrobe when I am stressed and get on my hands and knees and sniff around. So I did this, and the results were amazing. I could now survey the whole floor, and also I was less sweaty. After all, it was the wonderful month of June and Ariel's room is quite small and tends to be what members of the scientific community refer to as *a bit of a heat trap!*

After about fifteen minutes of sniffing, I'd gotten an excellent scent profile of the room (smelled like leftover Drunken Noodles from our special spot, mixed with notes of a marijuana brand called xx*StOneY bAlonEYYYYYxx*, mixed with a bit of the deodorant that all boys wear, certainly you know the name), but still, where was he?

I took a moment to stretch, paying special attention to the joints in my wrists and in my neck, and decided that I might as well check some of the drawers. It was useless! They were filled with Ariel's crack supplies since Ariel loved smoking crack before doing his homework and student grading, and of course there was about two thousand dollars in cash. I dug deeper, thinking perhaps I *just needed to look harder*, and came face-to-face with what appeared to be my lovely guy's DVD collection. This was confusing because the boys did not have a DVD player nor did they have a television, but it did not bother me because my Ariel is such a sweet, funny, and unusual gentleman. I was so happy for Ariel for owning a DVD where they play the NBA in outer space!

I began to feel the absolute strongest urge to hit myself in the head, hard, with one of Ariel's books. This was not unusual for me, and I had many techniques I liked to employ in the event that I wished to commit violence to the corporeal form of Reality. Frantically, I grabbed Ariel's pillow and put it in my mouth and began to gnaw on it. This was working. I no longer wished to hit myself in the head with a book or punch myself in the face. I was now calm. I was Zen. I was a beautiful, angelic floating entity and my vision became sharp and my brain began to soften.

"I am very relaxed!" I said to the ground.

I took my hands and put them to my face, and then put them on my stomach, and then put them on my ass. It was all there. Everything was intact. I felt ecstatic. I felt so deeply in my body that anything was possible. My guy would be home soon! And he would apologize and tell me that I was a wonderful, beautiful girl who deserves to be his lady. It would all be fine soon. I was so happy that I had learned the special calming techniques, although I could not remember where or when it was that I had gained this knowledge.

To celebrate, I took my hand and began to touch the organ. To my surprise, it was quite moist. I began to stroke it, and started to visualize the one thing I knew would do the trick. Using my imagination, I envisioned a stretched-out hand that slowly made its way to Reality's throat. It was a gloved hand. The glove was of gold and it was sequined. In this scenario, Reality was made to lay out on a white bed surrounded by red curtains. She wore a long dress wherein you could make out the outline of her breasts. The hand got closer, glowed in white light, and when it began to wrap around her little windpipe, all of the color in the room began to drain out. She pressed her hands together and laughed as if she were a baby or a parrot. And just as it became clear that she was going to die, just as the last drop of air was pursed from her throat, she began to hover above the bed.

It was then I realized I had cum all over myself, and Ariel was right there, standing in the doorway.

TEN

"Were you playing with your pussy without me?" said Ariel.

"Ariel! My sweetheart! Yes, forgive me for masturbating in your bed. I feared you were dead, seeing as you did not respond to my messages about the water park commercial that I did in Paramus, New Jersey," I responded.

"Oh," said my sweetie. "Water park commercial? Cool. Yeah, busy day. My students were so fucking annoying."

"That is ok, Ariel, but are you proud of me for my latest commercial?"

"Sure, whatever, Reality. Fuuuck. Anyways, whoa, I didn't even know you were going to be here. Honestly I'm really tired. It's been a lot of nights this week. Maybe you could just go home to your roommates? Or, like, you can sleep here, I guess, but I have, like, papers to grade."

I was so happy that he had given me the opportunity to stay the night. I felt the brightness and white light I had experienced while touching the organ all over again.

"Ha ha! No worries, Ariel! Yes I would love to sit here on your bed as you work. I will be seen but not heard! You could even put one of those dog muzzles on me if you wish! I am amenable to anything," I said with an air of unmistakable confidence.

I felt as if I were one of the many girlfriends of famous artists who would sit in the room as their true love wrote various texts and painted gorgeous images of fruits and breasts and odalisques, with a stunning rapier nailed to the wall. This was what it meant to be a girlfriend! The duty of a girlfriend was to smile sweetly while your boyfriend studies the good word. For many, this meant the Bible, for Ariel, this meant one of his texts on the Assyrian Empire.

"Ariel," I said sweetly. "May I get you something downstairs at the deli to help you feel nourished for your studies?"

"If you want. I'm not going to make you do anything. Ha ha. I'm not, like, your father," said Ariel.

"Ariel," I said. "As you know, I have a wonderful relationship with Mr. Kahn. He is where I get my nose and hilarious sense of humor. Also, it would be my pleasure to retrieve a snack for you at the deli!"

"Ok. Well, take some money at least. Can you get me one of those Demon NRG drinks, and, like, a pack of those sour gummies with the little children on them?" he said, brushing his long and luscious surfer hair out of his eyes.

"Ariel," I responded. "This would be my greatest pleasure! I will now go to the deli to obtain nourishment for your hard work."

Ariel bit his lip and looked down at his feet. He was wearing stripey shoes that were black and white. He took his hand and fished it around in his pants.

"Here's, like, twenty dollars," said wonderful Ariel. "Get yourself, like, one of those green smoothies you're always drinking. Also, relax, you're totally acting like Ashurbanipal—one of the worst kings of the Assyrians."

With my renewed sense of purpose, I began my sojourn to the deli. I was a bit disturbed by the Ashurbanipal comparison because I knew from Ariel he was known to be a hard-core, licentious tyrant, and me, I saw myself as a fey beauty. I didn't want to assign too much significance to it. If anything, I was seriously feeling like Tobias's dad, Tobit, sitting at the fig tree being like: Fuck, I am blind.

Anyways. It was quite the journey. Paradise was up three flights of stairs. Below the Joycean Boys, there was a sculptor named Medhi who spent all day listening to fractal constellations of sound and making the occasional phone call to a woman named Manon. They were always speaking in French and screaming. I knew this because one of my talents was that I studied the French language when I went to college. The sculptor did not care much for the boys and was always telling them to cool it with their instruments.

"Excuse me!" he would say. "If you would please to be quiet, I am very busy with the art!"

Below Medhi was a man named Luis who ran a pesticide company. Luis was very nice. He was always telling Ariel he was so happy to see that "wifey" was sticking around. Luis mainly dealt in bed bugs. One time I accidentally saw his butt crack.

I surreptitiously slinked down the stairs. It was unlikely that these men were there, but if they were, this was not the time for small talk. I was extremely busy getting My Love Ariel the required sustenance for grading the papers of his NYU students. Just as I walked past the door of Medhi, I heard a noise, and the door swung open.

"I am always telling you to please be quiet for my fine art!" said Medhi, his face obscured by the door.

He poked his head all the way out, to see who it was he was scolding.

"Oh," he said, "I am sorry for thinking it was one of these guys upstairs! I do not realize it was you."

"Me?" I responded. *He knew who I was!* I was becoming a fixture here at Paradise.

"Euh, oui," said Medhi. "You are the girlfriend of the guy who has *euh* the lisp and the lesbian haircut."

"Girlfriend???" I responded.

"Sorry, am I mistaken? Are you perhaps his seester?"

"I am his girlfriend! Et aussi on peut parler en français si vous voulez?" I responded confidently.

"Je savais pas qu'on avait une Française ici."

"Bah non, je viens de Upstate New York, mais en fait j'ai fait une année de ma licence à Paris," I said seductively.

"Ah trop cool. Tu veux boire un verre ou quelque chose? Vraiment tu es très bonne en français, franchement c'est um, hot."

It became evident that me and Medhi were flirting. After all, he was using the informal *you* with me! While I was enjoying getting to practice my French, it felt wrong wrong wrong to allow myself to be complimented by a man in this way, especially since I was on a journey for Ariel's well-being.

"Ok, c'est super gentil mais en fait il faut que je fasse un truc maintenant," I said to Medhi, coolly.

"Un truc? C'est un peu vague mais comme tu veux. Ah ha ha," he retorted.

"Oui! Ok, au revoir, Mehdi!" I said barreling down the stairs.

That was close! I thought to myself. I was shocked that I had allowed myself to flirt with another man! Let alone the wretched sculptor on the second floor! I decided to not give much weight to the interaction, even though at that very moment all I could think of was Medhi spreading me out on his worktable and poking me with his cock.

"Reality! Oh it is so good. J'aime trop ta chatte!" is what Medhi would say if he were railing me from behind on his worktable.

The French! France is a country of perverts! Perverts who love to fuck! I reminded myself.

I continued my march down the stairs. I simply would not allow myself to be distracted by any more neighbors. Certainly Luis would not distract me. I knew for a fact that he was often gone for the evening around this time. It would be no good at all if I were to run into Luis. The man had a gift for gab.

I approached his door. He was not in sight. This was excellent news. I began my final descent down the last few stairs. I let out a sigh. It was a huge relief to not run into Luis! I hopped down the next stair, and just as I landed on my feet, I heard the door swing open.

"Is that Ariel and the Boys?" said the voice of Luis. "Come in, I want to show you some baseball cards. I know you guys love baseball."

"Hi, Luis!" I responded. "In fact, it is Reality. I am on a journey for Ariel, actually. I'm going shopping!"

"Wait, what? Come in."

I peered into the chamber of Luis. It was very plain, and I did not see any baseball cards lying around. There was a computer that I think was about 386 years old as well as a filing cabinet and a spinning office chair with a dent where one's derrière goes. I dared not cross the threshold because of the presence of insects. This was having me seriously go bananas, the presence of insects. Additionally, fumes could come from the computer, thus rendering me incapacitated. They would be calling me WD-Reality. This is certain.

"Are you, like, buying him an assault rifle or something?" he continued. "Ariel would be the kind of guy to be, like, casually packing heat. He's shifty. Sorry. You need to watch your back around him. He seems like he would shoot up a school, no offense."

"Luis, you have Ariel pegged wrong! He is a member of the community," I said. "I bet you did not even know that my love works at NYU instructing our nation's youth on the Assyrian Empire. I'm actually off to the deli to pick up sustenance. He has a big night ahead of him, and I have taken it upon myself to nourish him."

"Girl, you are so fucking weird," responded Luis.

"Why weird?"

"I don't know. Don't take this personally but your vibe, it's off."

"Ok! I will work on this."

"Whatever. Wait, be right back."

I watched Luis go into his office and look inside the filing cabinets. This was very interesting. He pulled something out and walked back to me.

"Sorry about that, here's a baseball card."

I inspected it. Indeed, this was a baseball card. The baseball player had a bat made of what I believed to be a fine, oaken material.

"Frankly, you seem special needs to me, but knowing Ariel, that dude only fucks girls if they went to one of those fancy colleges in Rhode Island or Connecticut or whatever. Sorry. That was weird that I said that."

"It is true that I received my education from an exceptionally fine institution," I said. "In fact, that's where I met my roommates Soo-jin and Lord Byron."

"Ok. I literally didn't ask you that," he said.

Something I noticed about Luis is that he had beautiful, large brown eyes.

He was also strangely buff.

And his laugh was loud and full of mirth.

"Luis, I am wondering about the girls you mentioned," I said.

"Oh yeah. I mean, that's why my man is so sketchy, he's always having all these chicks over. I mean, not recently. But there are these girls who always have, like, a big ass and one of those funky haircuts and are wearing these little skirts. They look like lesbians, most of them."

I suddenly knew I needed to go. No. I knew too much. This would put a damper on my plans to be an amazing girlfriend to Ariel. I could already tell I was late. Also, it is considered improper to loiter. I was late and my face was beginning to freckle with tears. This was extremely bad. It had been years since it felt like this.

"You seem to have him tied down," said Luis. "That's nice. Dude might have some redeeming qualities after all."

An image of a knife appeared in my brain. It was true that I felt like death was arriving on these very plains of Gowanus.

"Luis. Thank you for the information but I absolutely have to go right now."

"Ok, girl," said Luis. "Door's always open if you want a drink or something."

Outside, where I stood now, it was a beautiful summer evening. Cars whooshed by me, and it smelled like a pleasing mix of hydrangeas and Colt 45. I spied the deli just down the street. I needed to channel my energy on the end product: my love, Ariel. It was no good for me to hear the facts from Luis. I knew that me and Ariel had not yet spoken of the terms of our courtship, but it was, in fact, distressing to hear. We both had lives before we met, yes, I was happy that it seemed as if Ariel had had a vibrant sex life before I entered the tableau. But I did not like this image of girls and girlfriends and ladies walking up the very stairs that I had just walked down. I imagined them in their skirts and dresses and sweatpants and lesbian haircuts, marching up to Ariel for sweet nooky.

Did Ariel pick me because I fit these categories? I did not know. I had mentioned so little of my life before to him. He did not need to know of the era where I played for each and every team.

It was then that I saw the little cat. She went by the name of Noor. She was the cat of the deli. A fine cat, I might add. She had beautiful orange fur, and soulful green eyes. She reminded me of my friend Watanabe, mostly because she had a little spunk and joie de vivre.

"Come now, Noor!" I said to the cat. "Pstt Pstt Pstt."

Noor moseyed her way up to me, and I pulled her close to my chest and she began to purr, calmly. *This is the life!* I thought to myself as I scratched behind her downy ears. It was ok that Ariel had many lesbian girlfriends before me! I felt calm and happy to know that my guy was so very experienced. This was one of life's great travails. Similar to the mantra: How do you get to Tammany Hall? Practice, practice, practice.

I hugged Noor closer, and it was then that she took her claws out and dug them deeply into my arm. I watched in horror as a brand-new bloody scratch appeared. I was clearly in hell! L'enfer! It was no good at all what was happening. I could feel myself collapsing into the sidewalk! I would die here! It was over for me!

The treacherous Noor scampered off. Here I was. Abandoned. I could feel my eyes growing heavy. I suppose it really was over for me. Over before it started. I pressed my face into the sidewalk as the light in my eyes went from red to gray to black.

In a soft, calm Germanic hum, the familiar voice thus spoke: *It is a place called Mount Nothing that you are meant to go ...*

In a tenor, in a baritone, in a contralto it continued and said: *And it is not Ariel who will be the boyfriend.*

This time he said in a whisper, more of a noise that trees make: *Go to the deli and figure the rest out later.*

ELEVEN

The deli was famous because no one was ever in it other than a man called Omar who always smelled of weed and was often watching wrestling videos on his cell phone. When I walked in, there he was. I could hear the soft buzz of beautiful WWE champions hitting each other on the head with chairs. *Wouldn't it be nice to be hit on the head with a chair?* said the familiar voice. It would! I thought about telling Omar this but then I worried he would think of me as one of those violent girls.

The deli really was one of the most gorgeous places I'd been to. The walls were a minty green color and there were mirrors all over the place. Also the lighting was amazing: it flickered on and off, like a strobe does. If it weren't for all the snacks, and the fact that Omar was behind a thick wall of glass to protect him from bullets, you'd think you were perhaps at a roller-skating rink where you do a waltz jump in a silver skirt. As I moved through the deli, I picked up my feet and did this very move. In my head I could hear thousands of individuals cheering. I do, in fact, think I was destined for this, to be lauded for my skills.

There was a magazine rack. I sauntered over to see if they had any copies of *Girlfriend Weekly*. To my surprise, it was there, hovering and bathed in a soft yellow light that I knew too well. Wow! Buona Fortuna! Amazing Luck. Score One For Reality! I took the magazine in my hands and flipped through. It was amazing, it glowed in my hands in a way that was holy. A religious text if thy name is Reality. As per usual, it was page after page of beautiful girls in there with all their advice on how to be perfect for your man. All the girls seemed to be smiling at me ♥♥♥.

I stopped at an advertisement that featured a buxom, zaftig young woman with long yellow hair and pretty blue eyes. She wore a white pinafore with a starched calico blouse underneath and a pair of penny loafers. And her smile was full of perfectly sized pearly whites. Of course this mademoiselle had plump-looking breasts. They were so soft. You could tell this from the photograph. I watched my hand hover over the breast and I imagined it in my hand, the way the nipple might pucker if I were to take my two fingers and really give it a good squeeze.

The text below read:

BE THE GIRLFRIEND OF HIS DREAMS

ZZZZvx ULTRA (XR)

A Dr. Zweig Altmann Drug

And there was a toll-free number at ⟨ℵ⊃ℶℵ⟩ that you could call right now if you would like to be in an advanced and paid drug trial courtesy of the revolutionary Dr. Zweig Altmann. I took my cell phone and saved the number. Just in case.

There wasn't time for this! I was here to buy my man his energy drinks. The double-chested fridge stood there and it was blinking at me as if it were sending me signals from another world. It was instructing me to make some good choices about my purchases. I could do this. I could forget what Luis and the familiar voice had said about Ariel dating all of those lesbians and maybe not being the boyfriend. All I had to do was pick out the perfect drink and then give it to him. And then give him a back rub and hear all about his day and tell him how he's such a special guy who deserves the world.

I got Ariel his favorite drink: Demon NRG X-TREME in purple. I grabbed one for myself, too, and took a sip. It was honestly really good and I instantly was like AHHHH SO HYPER. I also selected a snack he would like: corn chips. And one for me: a head of iceberg lettuce.

I walked over to Omar and he did not notice me.

"That's going to be a KO for Steve 'Übermensch' Yiannopoulos," said a voice from Omar's cell phone.

"Yeah, he's not going to recover from that one," said another voice. "Oh God, oh God, his nose is gushing blood. That's a broken nose for the former triple-crown champion!"

"I hate Greeks," murmured Omar.

I smiled at Omar and pushed my bounty toward the little slot beneath the bulletproof glass. The lettuce did not fit.

"Those fucking Greeks!" he said, louder this time.

"How much will it be for the food, Omar?" I said, avoiding his slander.

"I don't fucking know! Do you think I have every price memorized? Who do you think I am?"

"A friend," I responded.

"Eighty-five dollars," said Omar.

I pulled out my purse. I was not aware that Demon NRG X-TREME was so expensive.

"I'm kidding, miss," said Omar. "Sorry for my temper. Ten dollars."

I handed Omar the crisp twenty-dollar bill that Ariel had recently given me. "That's my boyfriend's money!" I told Omar.

Omar frowned at me and said, "Ok, miss," then hit a button on the computer which sputtered out change. It was like pirate money. Argh. Ariel would be so proud of me. I walked out, pocket full of doubloons. It was as if all was well. I was feeling really excited. Ariel would be so happy about the energy drink. And I was feeling pretty convinced I'd call the toll-free number. It was sounding pretty good to me. ZZZZvx ULTRA (XR). That was the name of the drug that could show a girlfriend all of her tricks! Also I wanted to *BE THE GIRLFRIEND OF HIS DREAMS*, obviously.

When I walked into Ariel's room, I heard a familiar noise. The sound of someone special striking a match. He was smoking his precious crack again in his beautiful little crack pipe.

"Ariel," I announced. "So sorry for the delay, but I have amazing news which is that I have all of the requested items."

"Hey, buddy," said Ariel, taking a hit from his crack pipe. "Glad you're back."

"Really?" I asked. "You're not mad at me?"

"Why would I be mad at you? You got me a weird energy drink and snacks and stuff, that's, like, actually super sweet. Come here," he said, motioning to his lap.

I climbed onto Ariel. He began to kiss me. I felt his hands all over my ass. He squeezed hard and then took his hand and spanked me. I loved having cracked-out sex with Ariel, I really did!

"Ariel . . ." I said.

"You look so good right now. You're all wired on caffeine. I bet you fucking loved that energy drink. You're going to be like a fucking jackrabbit on my cock."

Ok, now I was feeling like I was about to be condemned to Davy Jones's locker. Ok, now I was feeling like the child of the swamp haunt. These were normal feelings.

"Fuck," he said. "I'm so hard, baby, touch it."

I touched the cock of Ariel and it was indeed mineral-hard.

"Baby, you did this to me. Get on the bed. Come on, baby. Get on the bed. I want you to take this fucking cock and choke on it. You're going to be my little cumslut, aren't you, baby."

"Oh yes, Ariel," I said in the terrible whorish voice of a sexualized child as I wiggled out of my panties.

Ariel took out his cock and shoved my head down on it. It was always a pleasure to slob on Ariel's knob. I was being sloppy sloppy sloppy Reality going Up and Down.

"Yeah, so good. So good," said Ariel. "I want to do sex to you from behind."

I got on my hands and knees and spit up a little bit on Ariel's cock so it was nice and lubricated for anal.

In my mind the familiar voice was criticizing me and threatening to send me to Mount Nothing, so I blinked until he went away and cried with delight as Ariel shoved himself into my butt. I loved the feeling of being sliced open in the butt by a nice, girthy, yet not too large cock. It was so good inside of me—Ariel's cock, I mean. Surely you know what I speak of? Surely you, too, have come home from the deli only to be fucked in the ass by an Ariel or a Mike or a Timothy? I'm guessing at some point there's been an evening where you feel your entire asshole dilating for a dick to fit into it and then you start to cry a little bit but not because you are sad but because it hurts it hurts it hurts but in the way that you like the most? And that when you glance into his eyes, this Ariel, Mike, or Timothy, his pupils are like when the moon aligns with the sun in a certain way, creating a black hole in the sky at high noon?

Yes, whimpered my heart as he tunneled deeper inside of me. *YES!*

When you are having sex, where do you go? This time for me, it was not the glass coffin but instead the rings of Saturn. I was on a surfboard. I was wearing a blue dress. I was wearing a motorcycle helmet. It was lap after lap, veering past huge chunks of space debris. It was beautiful. It really was. It was so quiet out there, as well. I was not aware until this moment that when you are in outer space, outside of Earth's orbit, it is dead silent.

Ariel snapped back into focus. I could tell he was about to come.

"It feels *so good*, baby," said Ariel, thrusting deeper inside of me while taking his palms and rolling them over my small yet wonderful breasts.

"Arieeelllll," I said to Ariel.

"Ugh, baby, I am so fucking close," he responded.

"Ariellll," I said again.

"Yes, baby, come on, don't move, stop moving," said Ariel, flipping me over. "It's really hard for me to finish when you move like that. Fuck. Fuck. Fuck I'm coming, baby."

"Thank you, Ariel," I said as he ejaculated all over my stomach.

Ariel's eyes darted off. I wondered what he was thinking about. It was probably something wonderful, serene.

Above us, the overhead light flickered on and then off, on and then off. I took a deep breath. I was going to try this again. I had done what I was supposed to do. I had been amazing all evening even though it had taken me such a long time to arrive with the energy drinks and corn chip snacks.

"Ariel," I said, "I'm wondering if you've given it any more thought. About whether or not you want to be Boyfriend And Girlfriend."

Ariel breathed deeply out of his mouth and as he did this his hair fluttered.

"Oh shit, you're totally covered in cum. Here," he said sweetly as he handed me one long white gym sock.

"Ariel," I said, my face turning red. "I am serious. I really need to know the answer to this question."

"What? Oh yeah. Ok, sure."

And just like that, my heart, it whimpered again, and I felt relief wash over me, and I knew that the familiar voice was wrong and most importantly that I was about to become absurdly and insanely happy and it was all going to be so much different for me. And in the morning, I called the toll-free number. And it was the voice of a girl who responded and she said: "You seem like you're super pretty and totally sweet. How would you like to be one of the luckiest girls in the whole world?" And I said yes yes yes and before I knew it my life had become so beautiful.

AND NOW FOR A BRIEF INTERMISSION COURTESY

OF THE ZWEIG ALTMANN CORPORATION FOR THE

BEAUTIFICATION OF LAKE ANNECY 2

(A ZWEIG ALTMANN PROJECT)

REALITY (ephemeral, ageless beauty) sits in a white dining room in a little peridot-colored A-line dress when ARIEL (boyfriend, of course, and also a scholar) arrives home. REALITY is drinking a glass of green-colored juice with a straw. She slurps like this: *sllllurp*.

> **ARIEL:** Hey, babe, thanks for being here when I get home from researching the Assyrian Empire, specifically the destruction of Babylon under Sennacherib.
>
> **REALITY:** Love you, babe! All I've been doing today is making you an amazing meal at our home off the coast of Lake Annecy 2. It's pasta with chicken nuggets from the mall, and of course some Demon NRG X-TREME.
>
> **ARIEL:** Wow. I am in love with you and will always love you forever. Lake Annecy 2 is an awesome place that you [TURNS TO A STUDIO AUDIENCE OF BALD WOMEN WEARING WHITE DRESSES AND WINKS] will find out about soon. I promise this isn't irrelevant information to read after you all just found out about how our true love blossomed thanks to the cum sock.

ARIEL sits down at the dinner table and REALITY stands up, goes over to the stove, and lovingly puts pasta and chicken nuggets on a green plate which has smiley faces allllll over it.

> **ARIEL:** Wow, not only are you my girlfriend, you are a seriously good cook. [TURNS TO THE STUDIO AUDIENCE AND WINKS AGAIN]
>
> **REALITY:** Ha ha I love you so much! And I love the cum sock. I do this all for you and I agree this isn't irrelevant information for the middle of the book. Thanks to the other girlfriends, and ZZZZvx ULTRA (XR), I can be the perfect girlfriend for you.

REALITY winks and we can see that she is pregnant. She takes some more ZZZZvx ULTRA (XR) and rubs her belly. She looks off into the distance.

> **REALITY (to no one):** It was my whole life's work to be Ariel's girlfriend. Even before I knew what boyfriend-girlfriend meant it was true that this is what I had to do with my life. From a young age I dreamed of this insurmountable beauty that comes with being a vessel.

We cut to a sound stage in sunny Los Angeles, California. REALITY is in a little green dress with ruffles and has her left tit out so she can nurse her BABY. Her nipples, which were once pale pink, are now a brownish-reddish color. Across from her is THE ANNOUNCER, who sits there in a powder blue suit and looks just like REALITY'S old friend and agent JETHRO.

> **THE ANNOUNCER WHO LOOKS LIKE JETHRO:** The question everyone here wants to know is have you changed since you became Ariel's girlfriend and gave birth to his son Ignatius?
> **REALITY:** Thanks so much for asking this question, The Announcer who looks like Jethro, and um, well, hee-hee, the answer is, well, yes.

VOLUME TWO

ARIEL'S

When he finally agreed to be her boyfriend, the girl sighed like a baby bird. *Imagine now that the wings are fluttering.* The girl told all three of her friends. The girl called the toll-free number. *Imagine now that in a nightmare scenario the synthesis of these molecules will take on a cursed trajectory at a later date.* Her eyes welled with tears. *Imagine now that in the comfort of a dive bar photo booth they are doing kissing and holding hands.* She put her hand on her heart. He put a drink to her lips. *Imagine now that the heart, it too could sing. It could sing of the wonders of this love.*

Due to all of the above there was some talk of everything finally being perfect. There was talk that the tilt of the earth was finally just right. That the superbloom in the land of California would be ten times brighter. That la mer Méditerranée would shiver a deeper blue. That girls around the world would wear linen pants and charter boats. That boys would get down on one knee, holding the family amethyst. That cowboys in powder blue suits would scream across the sky in helicopters and land on the roof of a mall.

She was calm in her explanation of everything finally being perfect. "This is such an inspiring time to be alive!" she said. "All around me ordinary things are taking on verdant, ancient meanings! The strip of Gowanus where we live has begun to look like our very own Via Appia—the longest road in ancient Rome!"

The girl was acting like this for a really normal reason, actually. The reason is that she had arrived at a moment in her quest where there was a sense of relief.

That she would feel this sense of relief was decided from the moment she was bornth. Because for little girls when things go just right they are happy. They put you in a dress and everyone says hooray. And you are loved by many. And at the festival for the town you get to go on a parade float with your modern dance troupe. And when you do a good job they clap. When Ariel agreed to be her boyfriend it was like they were all clapping for her all over again and this was considered marvelous. Ariel, Ariel, Ariel. Everything had now become so easy, so wonderful, so perfect. Everywhere around the world they called her Ariel's. His girlfriend. At shows at the music venue, she was Ariel's. At the apartment with her roommates, she was Ariel's. At the train platform, in her perfect body, she was Ariel's. So now that she had relief, she had to solidify her position. She needed to make him love her. And this was one of the most difficult trials of her quest so far. Because you cannot force someone to love you. Even if you have the skills of a knight and the beauty of a princess who sits in the highest tower. You cannot force it. Instead, you must show kindness, grace.

So let's follow Ariel's as she bravely tries to make him love her. Let's follow Ariel's on her quest.

Read on, *man.*

IN WHICH REALITY AND ARIEL ARE NOW

BOYFRIEND AND GIRLFRIEND OFFICIAL

TWELVE

This was a peculiar time. Now that I was Ariel's, I had to make him love me. However, I could not force him. Because that could be dastardly. As a result, I was acting like a child with an affliction. But I was certain that the future would show itself if I took the marvelous pill ZZZZvx ULTRA (XR) and continued to read my favorite magazine, *Girlfriend Weekly*. And spending all of my days at Paradise was the way to do this—to ensure that I was working as hard as I could for my man.

This, of course, all happened because of the toll-free number. And the charming girl on the other line. ZZZZvx ULTRA (XR). I had been taking this for three months now. My brown waves had taken on a silky sheen. My lips had become a more scarlet shade of red. And my breasts, when Ariel took them in his mouth, they pointed with perfection. I dressed each day with an unmistakable confidence. Mostly, I wore dresses. Garments made of silk, of rayon, of muslin, all of which I had purchased using my water park money at a thrift store where there was a cashier named Valentina who was always quietly muttering slurs at me.

"Kike!" she'd say as she took my dollar bills.

"Whore!" she'd say as she took one of the gorgeous garments I'd purchased and placed it into a plastic sack emblazoned with a smiley face.

I was both a kike and a whore, so her words did not even bother me. And I was so in love. That was all I could focus on. It was like this now; all sound had become background noise. All human interaction outside of what I had with Ariel was now interstitial, plot points, a way to pass time.

In a word, my three months on ZZZZvx ULTRA (XR) had transformed me into the perfect girlfriend. I was so happy I could cry.

As a girlfriend, I now had relief. Security. This is like when you get a new job and they say that they will not eliminate your position unexpectedly. When shows at Paradise happened, I was introduced as a girlfriend. I got to join their special club. I became a girlfriend among a sea of girlfriends. When I saw them, the girlfriends, they'd recognize me as their own. They'd take off their hats and put them over their hearts when they saw me. They'd curtsy with their beautiful skirts. They'd put their hands on my shoulders. They'd whisper in my ear: *Hey, girl, how's it going?* When we ran into each other at parties we'd huddle in bathrooms and fix our makeup and talk about our guys. Me and the other girlfriends would say: *He gives me a run for my money but gee whiz am I so happy! Ha ha ha.*

It was magic every time.

Presently, Ariel and I were sitting in the living room of Paradise. Ariel was on the computer. He was writing a song. This involved him playing one of the pianos with one hand while he pressed and clicked on the computer's mouse with the other. As for me, I was making one of my zines. This was the other goal I had kept once I became Ariel's girlfriend. I had to continue to beautify the world. I had become a gorgeous thing; my output needed to match.

I took my pens and began to draw an image of my body on a piece of computer paper. It was, to be specific, an image of my ass. Lately, it had become afflicted with a disgusting skin disease known as jock itch. This is because Ariel and I were having so much amazing sex that I hardly had time to clean up. The other problem was that Paradise did not have a shower. If you were to shower, here's what you'd do: You'd take a mug, fill it with water, and baptize yourself with it. After, soap up a little bit, make sure to get underneath your armpits because those are the first to stink. Then you'll pour more water over yourself and voilà, you have taken a Paradise Shower. The other option is you can go to Aziz's apartment and say: *Aziz, please, I really need to take a shower. I smell literally so bad. I cannot take another Paradise Shower.* And then Aziz, Ariel's friend, rolls his eyes and is like: *Ok, I mean no? I mean Jesus, fuck, whatever.*

So anyways. I had jock itch due to the shower situation and it was going in my latest zine. I colored in the image of my body. Minus the jock itch, I looked like hot stuff. I really was about 84 percent more gorgeous because of being a girlfriend. Because it's art, I decided to take some artistic license with what color hair and stuff I wanted to have. Purple would do the trick. Purple with green streaks. As for my eyes: rainbow! It was already starting to look amazing!

Reality

it's ok to have
jock itch when you are
23 ♡

It was perfect. I was a natural artist. They had always said this about me. Art was another one of the skills that's great for a girlfriend to have, and fortunately I had a real knack for the arts. Traditional girlfriend skills are embroidery, painting, and dressage on a horse. Zines were a little outré for girlfriends, but me and my special guy, Ariel, lived in a community where being an individual with special skills was considered important.

I clicked off my pen. I was proud of my efforts. This was only the first drawing in the zine. There was going to be other stuff. Like, maybe a picture of Ariel riding a horse into the sunset? Or some facts about the Assyrians and their culture. Lately Ariel had been so busy with all of that. I mean school. He'd get back to Paradise and be like: "It's going to be a work night for me, Reality." Then he would shut himself in his bedroom and what I'd hear was the tinny sound of beautiful porno actresses getting totally reamed by some guy's cock.

None of it even bothered me. If he needed to take a break to jizz, so be it. I had no idea what it was like to be a learned scholar. I was far too concerned with being the best girlfriend I could possibly be. I was intent on being beautiful. I was waking up at 7:00 a.m. to run for one hour all around Gowanus. I was getting so fast. I was perhaps one of the fastest girls to ever run in Gowanus. As for food, it was mostly Demon NRG X-TREME because it made me feel like a psycho boss. I liked the chocolate flavor best, but occasionally would try the blue flavor, which had very interesting-tasting notes and recalled gasoline (I had never consumed gasoline before). I did eat other stuff. For example, sometimes I would go to the deli and ask Omar for one egg on a piece of homemade sourdough. I learned that this was a great breakfast to have so you can stay Proper and Thin in *Girlfriend Weekly,* which of course I was reading literally every day especially because it had successfully introduced me to the beautiful drug ZZZZvx ULTRA (XR).

When I purchased this delicious meal, Omar would usually glare at me and mutter to himself. Or, if he wasn't glaring at me, he was watching more wrestling videos on his cell phone. The reason for going to the deli was because Paradise didn't have a kitchen. So when you were hungry, it was either the deli or that pizzeria that also sells Thai food and bongs.

Why was tonight different from all the other nights? Tonight was a night that was different from all the other nights because Ariel had just turned in a chapter of his dissertation and he had finished all his grading, so he didn't have any homework to do. It was nice to watch him play one of the little pianos. He was such a talented musician. You will remember that Ariel was a child genius of the piano. I think in an ideal world, Ariel would want to be both a professor and a guy who plays in a rock 'n' roll band. He and Aziz had started a band and it was called Computer.

I looked up at Ariel from the ground. He was concentrating fiercely on his song. I didn't want to distract him, but I also wanted to give him a little kiss, so I got on my hands and knees and shuffled over to him like a baby. When I got to his ankles, I made goo-goo gah-gah whore eyes.

I pressed my lips to Ariel's left ankle and made a loud kissing noise.

"Agfhh," he said. "Reality?? Don't scare me like that."

"I just wanted to give you kisses, my sweet!" I responded.

"Oh, ha ha ha," said Ariel, getting off his chair and leaning in for a long kiss. His mouth felt perfect gracing the insides of my own. I felt so lucky. I had worked hard and felt as though I had earned this kiss.

"Reality?" said Ariel.

"Yes?" I responded.

"Want to come to this party with me later? Like, in a few hours," said Ariel. "It's at Brooks and Alma's apartment. I'm so tired but I feel like we should make an appearance. You love to party, right?"

"Party," I responded. As the word dripped out my mouth the room glowed in the romantic colors of Saint Valentine: purple, red, pink.

"You wanna go? I mean. You don't have to." Ariel laughed. "I mean you don't have to do anything. Ha ha ha. Sometimes I feel like you're my puppy, following me around. You're always here!"

"Yes," I said, picturing a dog version of Reality skipping through the fields of some remote and expansive steppe, perhaps in Patagonia. "I will gladly go to the party with you, Ariel!"

Ariel took a deep breath and stretched out his sexual and masculine physique. "Awesome," he said erotically. "I need to, like, go finish playing music and take a nap and stuff and then do you want to maybe meet me there?"

"Ha ha! Yes, of course! Alright, darling! I'll get myself ready for the party! I'll go back to my apartment and find the perfect gown to wear," I said, taking my drawings for the zine and putting them in a little plastic bag that we had gotten just yesterday at the liquor store. I couldn't wait. I could tell that it was going to be a beautiful evening full of mirth.

I really never went home anymore. It was the same when I walked in the door. Soo-jin and Lord Byron were reading the paper and a rock 'n' roll song was playing at a low volume. In the sink there was a big stack of bowls. It gave off a smell that was a mix of Greek yogurt and beef chili.

"Ugh," I said. "That smell is really gross."

Soo-jin and Lord Byron looked up, and then looked back down at the newspaper.

"You're one to talk. You're never even here anymore," said Soo-jin.

"Being so judgmental is not very becoming of you," said Lord Byron. "And besides, you literally do no chores, so why do you care."

I could tell that my roommates were mad at me, even though I disagreed with their rationale. It wasn't my fault I was always dragging dirt into the apartment and conducting various experiments. They were the ones who had said, "Reality, spend less time at the apartment." But I did not feel like arguing. I had big plans. Big business. I needed to be a beautiful girlfriend, a belle of the ball. I needed to look Drop-Dead Gorgeous For My Guy. It was hardly the time to discuss petty trifles.

When I walked in my room, it was chaos. I'm not sure who did it, but it was probably Soo-jin. Strewn around my room were various watercolor paintings and graphite drawings. I was happy that Soo-jin was fully realizing her artistic potential, but I was also a little bit concerned because I never gave her permission to just turn my bedroom into a kind of *salon d'artiste.* This was not Paris 1899! It was actually a hundred and twenty years later!

Besides Soo-jin's art projects, which were mostly pictures of Lord Byron in the nude, everything was how I remembered. There was my twin bed, which had a quilt that I took from a homeless guy who didn't need it anymore because he was going to die tomorrow. There was my lovely little lamp. A vintage photograph of my parents smiling and looking oh so happy on a camping trip. My diploma from Oberlin College in Theatre and the French Language with High Honors. A painting of a beautiful dog. A pile of my weapons: my seventeen knives and seven sticks I had sharpened with my knives.

I walked over to my wardrobe to select the perfect outfit. This was going to be tough because the name of the game was looking super gorgeous. I went on my cell phone and decided to see what *Girlfriend Weekly* had to say.

I typed into the search bar: *fancy outfit boyfriend date.*

I clicked on the first article. I knew immediately this would do the trick.

HOW TO LOOK REFINED YET GLAMOROUS AT
A BLACK-TIE GALA WITH YOUR BEAU

To look beautiful at a black-tie function, poise is a must. You must straighten your back so that way you have good posture. It is also essential to wear makeup. Foundation will even your skin tone. A little rouge on the cheeks and a simple lip color will give a sparkle in the eyes. Manicures? Yes. Choose a color that compliments your dress. Coral can be nice, sapphire, too. For your gown, maybe a neutral color. Something that will not distract from your man. If your boyfriend is an ambassador, perhaps wear the colors of the country he represents. If he is a lawyer, a copper-colored dress with short sleeves will suffice. Finally: parfum. Something regal. You can ask your local perfumer for his recommendations. Sandalwood is usually a wonderful scent.

I wished the article included a little information for what to wear if your boyfriend is an adjunct professor of classical civilizations and he sleeps on a cot at Paradise (#221). Nevertheless, I scanned my closet for options. So many of these dresses I had picked out with Emil at a store called Luxury Versailles 2002 Style Boutique. We were at the store and he was like, "Girl, try this one, it will make your fat ass pop." The ones which I had purchased from the thrift store were all in a garbage bag at Ariel's. And then I saw it, the perfect gown.

If the writers of *Girlfriend Weekly* saw it, they would have showered me with eternal praise.

The dress was a burnt orange and made of lamé. It had large sleeves that ballooned like the sails of a ship sailing the cool waters of the Bay of Fundy. The back was low. The bust was high. As I was not the girlfriend of a banker, it was crucial to not show much cleavage. And besides, it wasn't like I had much of it to begin with.

I did my makeup: a little rouge, not too much, no no no. Then, lipstick! The one I had was purple. I put on a dab of eyeshadow, it was green. And I sprayed on some more of my signature scent, the Printesa Sparkle Smell Perfume. I looked at myself in the mirror: I had magically transformed into Reality the Black-Tie Gala Girlfriend. Perfection.

It was time to go. I decided not to argue with Soo-jin about her artistic endeavors in my room since it was true that I was hardly ever there anymore. She and Lord Byron had since moved to the couch. I suppose I had been in my room getting ready for about twenty-two minutes.

"Soo-jin, I just wanted to say I'm actually not mad about the fact that you did some art in my room."

Soo-jin looked at me and said: "Girl, who dressed you? You look absolutely insane. In a bad way. Are you OK? You smell like alcohol and also a locker room. Is that guy you're dating abusing you? He really looks like a school shooter."

"It was I who did the art," said Lord Byron.

"Ok, nice! Well, keep up the good work," I responded. "Also, Soo-jin, I respectfully disagree. I actually read about how to be 'black-tie ready' in *Girlfriend Weekly*. The locker-room smell is because of all of the magnificent boys I now spend my days with! It must be hard for you to only get male attention from Lord Byron, who is not truly a lord! We all know he has the name Justin!"

"You're being a cunt," said Soo-jin. "I wouldn't make fun of people for assuming different aliases, if I were you."

This, in my opinion, was patronizing behavior!

"I hope a curse befalls you!" I said, closing the door behind me.

As I walked out the door, it seemed that maybe Soo-jin was jealous of my happiness. I mean, I know that she had found true love with Lord Byron, but I could taste her resentment. And besides, he really was not a lord! He was Justin Hopkins Jr. I suppose I took it a bit far with the curse comment, but her fiery wrath did not make sense. I am known to be a fiercely loyal individual with great skills. Recently my water park commercial had debuted on local networks and the royalties were coming in, hot. And according to Jethro, it was likely that they were going to put a photo of me on the side of New York City and New Jersey buses. In other words, things were looking up for my career. And, of course, when she referred to my boyfriend, Ariel, as looking like a terrorist who shot up elementary schools, what I think she was saying was: Ariel is a unique bad boy who often wore a leather jacket.

Ugh. I tried to not let Soo-jin's comments bother me, because it was so clear that she was jealous, but I felt sad. Me and Soo-jin had been through a lot together. Each time I got raped in college she was always so nice to me after.

I swatted away the thought right as the familiar voice started to materialize in my brain palace. I really did not want to talk to the familiar voice since he was always giving me bad advice.

DO NOT FORGET WHO ARE YOUR TRUE FRIENDS, it said even though I thought I made it really clear I was not feeling chatty. *THE YOUNG TURKS WILL DECEIVE YOU!* it continued. Whatever. It was time to go to the party.

THIRTEEN

YOU ARE ASSERTING CLASS AT THE FUNCTION

When you arrive at the black-tie gala, it's important to make small chitchat and to seem quite engaged with whatever it is you speak about. If another lady in the crowd tells you about a pie she made for the local church, be sure to ask her what flavor, and whether or not she received smiles from the priest. If a gentleman asks if you and your boyfriend have plans to get married, go ahead and say, yes, we are so happy together! If you're asked what literature, music, and film you've recently enjoyed, try this handy guide:

1. I have recently read A Lady's Guide to British Country Living
2. Opera
3. A documentary about the war

I was the belladonna of the ball. I was armed with a Rolodex of conversation topics on how to be a bonne vivante courtesy of *Girlfriend Weekly*. But first, champagne. It was time for a coupe, something to make me approachable, yet somehow bourgeois. With champagne I'd find the other girlfriends and we would chitchat about our boyfriends and how lovely we felt in their arms.

Oh, I knew Ariel would be so proud of me. He was running late, he always was, so it was really important that when he arrived, I was happy and occupied. Another fact about boyfriends is they like it when you show them that you're really independent, that you don't need them or think about them and when they're not present you are not wondering to yourself if maybe they got hit by a New York City bus where there is a photo of a girl named Reality on a waterslide. I had learned a lot.

The table where drinks were served was white plastic. A table for playing cards if it is summer and you are sitting in the backyard of some splendid Basque villa, perhaps drinking a little cup of Txakoli. On the table, there was a bottle of tequila, a bottle of vodka, a bottle of rum, a carton of orange juice, and a bag of potato chips. *But where is the champagne?* I wondered inside of my head.

Beside the table, there was a girl. She had green hair. The hairstyle was a mullet. She wore a yellow T-shirt with a picture of a rabbit on it. Beneath the rabbit was the sentence: *CUTE BUT CRAZY!*

"It appears there is no champagne here at the party," I said to the green mullet girl. I noticed that beside her hand, there was a book. It was a large book and it was by a famous author. On the cover there was a man wearing a menacing top hat. When I looked at the man it seemed as if he were making unsparing eye contact with me.

Hello, Reality, the menacing top-hat man seemed to say. I blinked. The green-haired girl was still there!

"Nice eyeshadow," she said.

"Are you a scholar? I ask this because of your book. Also, I am wondering if you happen to see any champagne. I really would love some champagne."

"What?" asked the girl. "Are you high on drugs? Who are you?"

"Reality, Reality Kahn. Mainly I'm Ariel's girlfriend. But I'm also an actress for water park commercials, and I make fine art."

"Ariel?" she asked as she took the vodka and poured it in a cup, all the way to the tippy top. "As in like, Koffman? Assyrians Ariel Koffman?"

"Yes, the very same," I said. "And I'm assuming if you recognize his name you are one of the other girlfriends at the party?"

"Girlfriend? Ha. No. No way. Wow, you're such a trip. He's right, you have a really nice body. Look at that little ass. That motherfucker is such an ass man," she said. "Ha! Sorry, I can't do this right now. I'm kind of drunk and you're, like, ambushing me. I need a smoke."

I watched in horror as the girl walked over to a corner where, standing alone, she took a cigarette from her pants and lit it up. She was muttering to herself and blowing smoke rings like she was a detective in a detective novel. Who was this woman? She seemed to know a lot about Ariel. It didn't necessarily bother me because Ariel is one of the most interesting men in the world and also this was a convivial evening of friends Ariel met back when he was a Yale Man. What was strange is that she knew so much about me.

I decided to go mingle.

It was an attractive crowd at the party. No one was really dressed for black tie, but many were dressed for a good time. I moved from room to room in search of champagne and good conversation. While I didn't find champagne, I did find an original drink, a cocktail of the house. It was called Godzilla, and it was made for me by a man with a tattoo of grapes on his bicep.

"It's vodka, rum, and apple juice," he said as I stared at the grapes tattoo. "I call it Godzilla because it's like 'AAHHHH!!! Me dinosaur.'"

I smiled and consumed my drink. It was very alcoholic, and I could tell instantly that I was going to be quite inebriated. I wished there were some canapés around, but seeing as there was no champagne, I couldn't get my hopes up that there would be much in the way of bite-size delights for waking up the palate. *Where was Ariel anyways*, I wondered, checking my cell phone. No texts.

I looked around and wandered into a bedroom. In case you were wondering: Ariel was not lying on the bed with a rose in his mouth to the tune of flamenco music! But what I saw instead was equally compelling: it was a group of girlfriends. I could tell instantly based on their body language and their intonations. They spoke and it was like hearing fireflies on a summer night or an aria by a commanding soprano. And they were so beautiful, the girlfriends. They all had long hair. Wavy. Pin-straight. In a bun. In braids. They drank sips of wine and tossed their heads back to laugh. *Ha ha ha ha*, they all said in unison, so musically. And they were so well dressed, too. They crossed their legs in cigarette pants and pinafores. *These are my people*, I thought. These were the girls who made our boys so happy. They were responsible for being around to fuck. They opened the door after baby came home from a long hard day at the office and said: "Hey, honey, I'm going to suck you dry now. Also, I love you!"

When you see girlfriends, it's important to consider your approach. You don't want to surprise or disturb them, for example. You want to appear natural, cucumber-cool. As if you've always been there. You have to prove you're just like them. It's helpful to strike up a meaningful conversation about something that everyone knows about. Possible topics of conversation include what country club you all belong to and the best kind of rental helicopters.

You also might want to go to the powder room and freshen up. It's stressful to be talking to a gaggle of girlfriends and then realize that your eyeshadow is all smudged.

"Yoo-hoo!" one of them said. I suppose she noticed I was considering my approach.

"Come over here!" said another one.

"Hey, lady! You look like one of us," said a third.

Cautiously, I walked over. I noticed that the girlfriends were all draining their glasses. "Hey, girlfriends," I said to the group. "Hey, babe!" they all responded. "You look like you need some wine," said a girl with long brown hair.

The girl grabbed my waist and smiled at me so very affectionately. She had the eyes of Bambi and her breath smelled like a mix of wine and peppermints. "You're literally so cute, babe," said the girl. "I'm Stefie. I'm Alexi's girlfriend." I watched as Stefie took a bottle of red wine and proceeded to put it in her mouth and peel off the layer of foil around the bottle's neck. "Ok. Literally amazing. You must be Ariel's new beau. So awesome. It's amazing what he's doing with the Assyrians and stuff. Did you meet Katie yet? She has, like, green hair. Total sweetheart. She used to date Ariel. I mean, like, they were fucking on and off for like two years. You'd seriously love her. You guys have so much in common. Ugh. Oh my God, I miss Alexi. He's in the other room with the boyfriends. I think they're playing poker or something." Poker. Was this a game Ariel liked to play? Maybe he had arrived, unbeknownst to me, and was in there right now! I sent him a text. God, I hoped I would see him soon so he could give me a kiss. So that he could say: "You are my girlfriend and are extremely awesome. I haven't seen you all night because I was testing you!"

Stefie turned to me and grabbed my shoulder.

"Come with me to the bathroom so I can fix my makeup."

Like a little lamb, a safely grazing sheep, I followed her oh so sweetly. Doucement, doucement.

In the bathroom it was even more girlfriends. If I had to guess there were maybe seventy-five of them in there. They all sat around in the bathtub shaving their legs and on the toilet drinking wine and smoking cigarettes and touching up their makeup. They were so beautiful. It was really so amazing to be with them. I was so honored to be recognized as one of their own. This is what it was all about. It was the feeling of being a siren among sirens. A Sabine to be claimed by a Roman youth.

"Hi, ladies!" said Stefie. "Ok, so this is Reality and she's a girlfriend just like us. Make her feel at home while I fix my mascara. It's seriously starting to bleed. Racoon vibes, am I right?"

"Take off your top, babe," said a girlfriend with blonde hair who was in the bathtub. "You'll be so much more comfortable."

Not wanting to be rude, I disrobed. This was really escalating! The girlfriends surrounded me, taking their hands and putting them on my breasts. "How long have you been a girlfriend for?" said a girlfriend with black hair wearing dark purple lipstick. "If I had to guess, it's been about eight months. Your body is beginning to grow soft, yet the skin around your face remains taut. One day you'll be soft all around like us. The ideal girlfriend has a body that says, *You can put a baby in me whenever.* Do you want to be like this?"

I smiled and nodded. I imagined myself wearing a calico-printed housedress, sitting at a little picnic table in the backyard of a Vermont farmhouse. In this vision, I was fat and happy with Ariel's baby doing backflips inside of my tummy.

"Have you heard about the famous Dr. Zweig Altmann?" said the girl with the black hair.

"Why yes!" I responded. "I'm a fan of the doctor's work and I myself have been on the ZZZZvx Ultra (XR) regimen for a few months now."

"Zweig's a goddamned certified medical genius, good thing you called the toll-free number," the girl said. "Oopsie doopsies. Hee-hee. Pardon my français. Girlfriends don't swear unless they are trying to seem at ease in group settings. Anyways, glad to hear you're on one of our Dr. Altmann's little pills. You haven't been taking it for long enough. You should double your dose. You should spend more time with us. When girlfriends stick together, we all can be better at our jobs. Don't you want that?"

"Ha ha! It would be so amazing to spend more time amongst gorgeous like-minded individuals so we can all help our special guys," I said in a relaxed and convivial tone.

"That's the spirit," the girl said, unzipping my dress all the way down.

"Super hot," she said, taking a finger and putting it in the organ. "Are you always this wet?"

"Hee-hee-hee," I giggled.

"Zweig's going to love you."

"You're so gorgeous. You're totally on your way!"

The girl zipped my dress back up, pulling my ass into her crotch and grinding on it a little bit.

I looked at the mirror. Stefie was there, closing the tube of mascara and batting her lashes.

"So glad you two ladies had a chance to meet," she said, pointing to the girlfriend with the black hair and lipstick. "Mallory's doing really amazing work for us. She's so amazing. We really love her. She's kind of the main girlfriend around here."

"We're literally so happy you're here, Reality," Mallory whispered into my ear.

I blinked and shivered. How many people were actually in here? Just being around my fellow girlfriends made it as if the world were a pearl and I was walking through bivalves. It made me feel like we could be an army of hundreds, millions, trillions, even though our numbers were far less. Everything was so shiny. It was true that I was becoming more docile than ever. People gave me more wine and I became so sweet. When I was asked how I was doing, I did this amazing and polite little giggle. When asked where Ariel was, I'd say: "Herr Professor! He shall be arriving so soon." The girlfriends would pass by me and they would kiss me on the cheek and tell me I was looking so good in my dress and then we would grasp each other's hands and it was like this fluttering feeling and inside my brain it was calm calm calm.

There was a ring at the doorbell and then my sweet arrived. Ariel. I was doing this all for him. Self-determination is like when you have a boyfriend and then you make it your goal to do everything possible to be a perfect beacon of goodness. I decided I would not bother him. I would be there for him, yes. But I would give him the space he needed to have thought-provoking conversations with his fellow guys. And when he was ready for me, well, I was on my way to becoming so perfect, courtesy of ZZZZvx ULTRA (XR).

He put his coat on the coatrack. He rustled around in a plastic bag to reveal that he had some beer. I watched in awe as he slicked back his mop of brown waves. And then it was so wonderful when he bent over to tie his shoelaces. I could smell him from across the room. And it was pure heaven as he began to chat with the men. It was my favorite part when the boys stood there drinking their beers. It was all ambient language to me, whatever it was they were saying. It did not concern me. And when I saw Katie approach Ariel, and then put her arm around his waist, all I thought about was how lucky I was. I really was.

I was so lucky.

VOLUME THREE

VALERIE

When she came back from the party the girl sighed like a baby bird. *Imagine now that the wings are fluttering.* The girl collapsed onto the bed. The boy wanted to fuck. *Imagine now that in a nightmare scenario this is a bed from which you do not wake.* Her eyes welled with tears because she couldn't figure out how to say no thank you!! *Imagine now that the phone is off the hook, that it is buzzing buzzing buzzing.* She couldn't say no thank you!! because she loved him. *Imagine now that the foreign invaders inside of your corporeal form are doing this because they love you! They love you! They love you, they really do.* And she loved him in a way where you just can't say no. You just can't.

Due to all of the above there was some talk of the boy whispering into her ear, "You're so drunk, it's kind of hot."

She was calm in her explanation of why she was drunk. "Pffffgh-hhh," she said. "That feels great, Ariel!"

The girl was doing this for a really normal reason, actually. The reason was she had learned a very important and special lesson.

Here was the lesson: sometimes when you love someone so much, you have to lie down and take it. Even when you get too drunk at the party because your boyfriend shows up two hours late and talks to some jeune fille with a green mullet instead of you. You have to take it in order to be the greatest girlfriend of all time. You have to take it and shut your eyes and picture what a pink Jeep under the Manhattan Bridge would look like if someone threw a car bomb at it. You have to clean the cuts off your thighs with yellow Dial soap.

This is all part of the quest. This is how you become a hero. This is how you save the day. This is how you get your hero's cape.

And she looked so perfect when she lay there and took it. She really did. She looked so perfect.

That she would learn this very important lesson that she would do anything for him was decided from the moment she was bornth. Because when a mommy and a daddy love each other so much what they do is they touch belly buttons and then in nine months there is a baby and they name her Valerie Estelle Kahn and in the sky it is the Hale-Bopp Comet and the baby's destiny is to be a girlfriend. Valerie is a happy baby and there are no issues. She talks early, says the word *grandpa*, followed by *shoes*, because of her love for beauty. Then after her first words she walks and because this is a small town in the Adirondack Mountains there is a lot to see. Baby Valerie picks up salamanders with her bare hands and she puts them on a rock and gives them names like Rebecca and Timothy. For dinner it is chicken nuggets and pasta followed by a scoop of ice cream and Mommy and Daddy are really proud of her because she is a good girl and she is doing exactly what she is supposed to at that age, which is playing games like Patty-Cake Patty-Cake Baker's Man and Red Light, Green Light and Mafia. The last one is where there is one little boy or girl who is in the mafia and everyone has to guess who and there is also someone named God. Little Valerie made a few close friends, and she is a late reader with a low quantitative IQ, but her teachers really like her and on the weekend Mommy and Daddy would read her chapter books where a little girl or boy saves the day, and her first crush is a little boy named Ian, and he is her crush because he helps her sound out the words and this makes Valerie blush. The winter is always icy cold because it is the mountains where she lives so little Valerie learns how to ski and ice skate. If you're wondering about the jobs, well Valerie's daddy is a doctor at the local air force base and Valerie's mommy teaches kids who are special needs and it is a comfortable childhood in a 2000s lived but illusory with a brick schoolhouse on top of a hill and the swoosh of a calico-printed party dress in a sea of small towns with New Testament names and vacations to Hollywood, Florida, where Grandpa and Grammy live and they feed her fried clam strips and watch as she makes sandcastles and her grandpa takes her on his lap and teaches her how to whistle and on the TV chubby blonde girls with names like Madison and Jenny are abducted into white slavery and Mommy is crying because of the corruption and the hurricanes and the wildfires and the military juntas and the blast that has turned a business area into a crater as if on the moon and she puts little Valerie on her knees and says to her, *Wow, I feel like I was twenty-three like it was yesterday! In the late 1980s everyone was always drinking cosmos!* and in the winter it is three feet of snow and the children in the town build beautiful snow forts and drink hot cocoa and then they all go to the skiing hill and they go down the slopes and Ian is there and he helps Valerie down the mountain and now they are age thirteen and they call it pastoral in some parts of the country but to Ian and Valerie the day of the week is Saturday and that is what makes it remarkable. Sometimes Valerie comes home from school and she and Mommy make cookies and when it is Passover Valerie's grandpa and grammy come up from Hollywood, Florida, and Grammy takes Valerie's hands and shows her how to take walnuts and apples and turn it into a Jewish salad and Grammy hugs Valerie and so she smiles.

The real tragedy is when the family dog named Reality attacks a little girl in a white dress and they have to kill it with drugs and Valerie cries and then in high school Valerie gets a short haircut and listens to indie rock 'n' roll on her iPod Touch and googles pictures of Alexa Chung and all the boys talk about Odd Future and smoke weed in the parking lot of the high school and one day she sees a shooting star at summer camp in New Hampshire and goes to New York City for the weekend if only for the freedom of wearing a tennis skirt in Central Park and the first time Valerie ever kisses someone it is to the song

"Chicago" by Sufjan Stevens and they are at a bear-infested campsite and to commence kissing the girl who is a prominent WASP named Kansas slaps the joint out of her mouth and not long after Valerie becomes convinced she will be saved by something called *Revolution Girl Style Now!* and back at home Ian and Valerie become best friends and it's not weird that Ian finds true love with a man named Tommy who he met chain-smoking in front of the VFW on School Street and they do anal in his Datsun and Ian and Valerie go to the shopping mall in Queensbury where they try on sweaters and eat at Paradise Grill and Ian tells her all about this and how he takes Tommy's cock in his ass and then Tommy goes home to his wife and two kids and how he served in the Iraq War and honestly it's not that tragic Tommy is always saying how it's sexy to have a secret and how the whole point of having a second life is that You Don't Owe It To Anyone To Give It All Away.

And Valerie agrees. She thinks it's so cool to have a secret, and when she gets home after the mall she writes: *Dear Diary One Day I Hope To Have A BF Just Like Ian's Iraq War Veteran.* And underneath this she draws a picture of a guy holding a gun. A gun! And one day when she gets home from the mall what happens is she opens up her computer and goes on a website and it is boys boys boys boys boys on the website.

And so here is how Valerie gets sooo weird: She gets waterboarded in a CIA black site; she gets chased through the woods by a bunch of guys wielding steak knives, it is knaves who finish the job; she's the babysitter and when the kids go to bed she hears a *knock knock knock* at the door and suddenly it is a man in a mask and he tells her the end is near; she falls into the San Andreas Fault line; she gets pushed off the side of a building; she is walking down a dark, empty street and so a bunch of guys take their dicks out and start saying terrible, terrible things; she steps on a Soviet land mine; she licks an American IED; she takes nine Benadryls and then throws her body in a ditch and gets hypothermia. She walks through her college dorm room listening to the same Radiohead song over and over and over again while contemplating killing herself, the flickering of the vegetable knife, the steam of the washer they call Hobart. A pack of feral dogs is unleashed, and a Rottweiler drags her by the ankles back into its den. Died in Treblinka, survived Pompeii! Telemarketers in steel-toe boots, pedaling wares. The teacher is a rapist, Daddy's bad bad bad bad. Girlfriend, you could get totally decapitated; girlfriend, you're seriously about to get dragooned; an arms dealer puts her in a dog crate and she wakes up on the island of Crete in a bikini on a couch; her remains are discovered by a street urchin named Tiny Timothy and it's his duty to scatter her ashes somewhere beautiful, like Mount Kilimanjaro or Ardèche or Marin County.

And when this happens there is peace in the valley, by the lamb, by the lion. And when this happens there is a cowboy in a powder blue suit and he *winks* at her. The cowboy in the powder blue suit tells her, *Go out on the floor and organize the merchandise.*

So here's the thing about Valerie: she is actually a genius and a street fighter with a heart of gold and she always bounces back superfast.

So here's the thing about Valerie: when she lay there and took it she was *grateful.* She *smiled.*

Read on, *man.*

IN WHICH AFTER LEARNING AN IMPORTANT
LESSON WE FOLLOW REALITY ON A
LAST-DITCH ATTEMPT TO BECOME THE
GREATEST GIRLFRIEND OF ALL TIME

FOURTEEN

This was a peculiar time. I had to be the greatest girlfriend who ever lived. I was acting like a child with an affliction. I had neglected my duties. I had learned an important lesson and this was a harder pill to swallow than my all-time favorite drug ZZZZvx ULTRA (XR). But I was certain that the future would show itself if I worked hard for my man. I needed to be the greatest. The greatest girlfriend. The best there ever was. And Stefie's apartment was the place to do this—to realize my potential.

This, of course, all happened because of the party with Ariel. Because Stefie had brought me to the bathroom and introduced me to my crew. The girlfriends of the hour. Les filles du calvaire. The girls on their horses. And in their dresses! Stefie was one of them. And she was going to help me fix all of my problems. She would show me the true way. She had even gone so far as to contact me, to share her intention of becoming my aide-de-camp on my peregrinations, via text message:

Hey Reality xx So cool seeing U at the party!!! Lets drink wine sometime ;-) I WANT 2 HEAR EVERYTHING!!!!!!! BTW this is Stefie. PCE.

Everything was about to change. I was more ready than ever. And I was delighted that she wanted to drink some wine "sometime." Now this was a friend for life. Unlike Soo-jin and Lord Byron, who kept sending me texts saying stuff like: "You're being really selfish, Reality," or "Can you please come over and deal with that nasty-ass pile of underwear in Lord Byron's art studio." Meanwhile Stefie was waiting for me. Goodness me! The thing about us girlfriends is that we have kind of a psychic connection. We can read each other's minds. This is why as soon as I received this missive, I was on my way.

I knew where Stefie lived because she told me at the party, that fateful evening where my life became perfect. It was a neighborhood called Bay Ridge and she said she lived there because it was cheap cheap cheap. This is a storied endroit. Me oh my. She also mentioned that her apartment was above a world-famous Italian bakery where they sell many types of crusty yet delicious bread. Using context clues, I determined that her apartment was above Russo's Italian Bread Bakery.

When I got to the bakery, I asked where I could find Stefie. Part of me wondered if she lived in one of the ovens, keeping warm with the help of charcoal and semolina. It was a lost cause. The woman at the counter was just standing there tapping her extremely long acrylic nails that featured small crystals in the shape of hearts. "I do not know who this is," said the woman. "This is a family bakery. You do not find girls who live here. Not a whorehouse or nothing. My hands are clean. My husband is in jail for RICO charges but not me. He is one sick fuck, I will tell you this much. Maybe you go across the street to DiNapoli's and you see if they got any whores living there. They have issues over there, for serious."

I had a feeling that I was being misunderstood by the woman at the counter so I bowed my head to show I was appreciative of her time and then tried to see just where Stefie might live. It was possible that she lived in DiNapoli's, but the rational Reality said: No, c'mon. *Check the door next to the bakery.* And just like that, next to the building there was a door, and next to it, a series of buttons indicating who lived where.

I scanned for Stefie's name. And presto! There it was. Stefana Alana Bianchi. Apartment 3. I buzzed. She answered.

Stefie's apartment was a girl's paradise. Not to be confused with Ariel's house, of course. What I mean is that everything was pink and purple and it smelled like roses and honey and nicotine. On the wall, there was a pink neon sign that said STEFIE. On her pink coffee table, there were magazines about shopping and fine art. She did not appear to have *Girlfriend Weekly*, so naturally I wondered how she had learned to be so skilled at being Alexi's. She pulled a pretty pink bottle of wine out of the fridge and began to drink straight from it. In her hand that wasn't holding the bottle, she fished around in her pink jeans until she produced a pack of cigarettes and a lighter. I watched with delight as she lit one and drank from the bottle at the very same time. I took a mental note: *A girlfriend must multitask.*

"I'll have a cigarette, too, Stefie," I said with an appealing smile and tone of voice.

"Sorry, it's my last one," she responded.

Stefie's attitude seemed a little different from when we first met, but I tried not to take it personally. She was really smart and she had an important job outside of being a girlfriend, which was being an intern. "Don't ask me what my internship is, I'm not telling you," she said when I asked her to elaborate. "The internship is why I'm busy, and not usually around for girls like you to just drop by and ask me for favors. My time isn't free. I went to school with Ariel and all those boys, which means I'm really smart."

I was in a good mood. I was feeling assuaged. Finally, Stefie continued to drink her wine and eventually allowed me to have a little cup of my own. "So greedy," she said, as she poured some wine into a glass. "Are you Jewish?" I smiled and said yes! How could you tell? Stefie got close and stroked my deviated septum. "Alexi is coming over in a bit and I need to get ready for him. You know what I'm talking about?" she said, sticking her tongue out. ZZZZvx ULTRA (XR)! Of course. The effects on Stefie's body had been great. As for her mind, well, it was kind of hard to tell since Alexi wasn't around, but she was really beautiful and soft. I decided that the reason she was acting so differently from the party was that she was waiting for her man and this was considered a stressful time.

"Anyways," Stefie said, lighting up another cigarette. "As I was saying, I'm super busy with my internship. I work forty hours a week at it. Top secret. I had to sign an NDA. And don't ask me what it is, by the way. Don't ask me about my internship, please."

I took a sip of my drink and smiled. It was so nice to have a new friend who really understood what I was going through. She was working so hard to make Alexi's life better and happier. I bet she was amazing at sex as well and Alexi was always patting her on the head after the blow job was done.

"You're being super quiet, it's weird," said Stefie. "How are you enjoying the new dose of ZZZZvx ULTRA, by the way?"

"Hi, Stefie," I responded. "I'm so glad you asked! It's going super well. It's only been a few weeks, but I'm feeling really good and can already notice some improvements in the bedroom and otherwise. For example, I have stocked Ariel's fridge with all of his favorite Demon NRG products and, additionally, my ass has become the perfect size."

Stefie smiled at this information. Then she put her hand on my thigh.

"Reality, you ever do stuff with girls?" she asked.

"Yes, I do! For example: manicures, pedicures, brushing each other's hair, going to the mall, and talking about our boyfriends."

"No, I mean, like, sexually," she said.

When I tried to think about it, what I saw was a Catherine Wheel of limbs on fire. It was breasts and hands and genitals of all kinds, but it was more or less a single organ that moved together. And it did not have a face and it did not give me love it just was a feeling and when I looked for the center it was loud, loud, loud. Lots of laughter and yelling and clapping and cheering. An indistinguishable sucking of the event horizon where it is girls with the names of Midwestern states and boys with shaved heads and a piercing on the eyebrow and three-ways and four-ways and doing it on a car on a bus on a train on a plane and in a Dodge Charger idling in a field somewhere past Far Rockaway where the CD playing is the sounds of waterfalls and asteroids and beams of sun and the cowboy in the powder blue suit says, *Darling girl, have a little blow* *snort* and this made me like a trained seal in one of those amusement parks where the seal does things like play with a red rubber ball on the tip of its nose. So I went further and further, it became very dark and it was an ice-cold breeze and suddenly I was alone and I did not know where I was or what was going on. I only lay there and I smiled so graciously on the bed until it descended upon me, this darkness, and there was nothing left and when I touched my face I noticed that I had become a giant wound.

But what I said was: "Ha ha, I'm not a prude! Of course I have."

"Ha ha, nice!" she responded in a perky voice. "You should be receiving an invite soon."

I readjusted my dress. Stefie put my glass of wine to my lips. I noticed that the STEFIE sign was flickering on and off very fast.

"An invite? To where? I am sure this will be oh so fun," I responded.

FIFTEEN

I agreed to meet Emil at the grocery store because he wanted to buy magazines and we used to go there together all the time. It was a beautiful place, the grocery store. And it was so large. There are not many large grocery stores in NYC, but this one was really huge and contained aisle after aisle of everything you could possibly need. For Emil, this meant magazines with the latest gossip. For me, this meant trying to find my favorite rag, *Girlfriend Weekly*, and perhaps a bottle or two of Demon NRG X-TREME.

Emil looked like his normal self. He wore a pair of red B-ball shorts and a giant T-shirt that advertised cigarettes. On his feet, a pair of sandals that you often see if you are in a locker room at the fitness center. He was looking very handsome, and certainly was aware of this fact. Perhaps this was on purpose, given our sexual past.

"I have so many text messages," said Emil. "They're from all the girls who want me."

I smiled and patted Emil on the shoulder. We were supposed to be talking about how I was really beautiful and totally transformed by girlfriendhood and also that I had been on ZZZZvx ULTRA (XR) and it was starting to really work. I wanted him to tell me that I simply looked divine yet he continued to talk about the girls he found out about on websites.

"I was talking to Sarbjeet about it when we were smoking weed and he said I should really go out with this girl. Look," said Emil.

The girl was from a website that promoted alternative relationships. She called herself a rope bunny and wore her hair in terrible, whorish pigtails. And her titties were poking out of her shirt.

"Emil," I said in a kind and considerate tone of voice. "I'm going to be honest and tell you that this girl looks like a total slut. This is not girlfriend material."

"This bitch is craaaazy!" said Emil, to no one in particular. "She's off the chain!!!!!!"

I smiled at Emil, and watched as he picked up a magazine and flipped through the pages.

"There's a lot of insane shit going on. We're seriously fucked. Actresses are doing insane things. Same with the actors. Wait. Ok. I'm sorry. I'm being so rude. Ha ha. For serious. How are you? You look a lot different. Like, I never see you anymore."

"Hi, Emil. I'm glad you actually brought this up. So I'm a whole new person since I've found love. Ariel's really so amazing to me. He's my Best Friend. And I'm doing everything I can for him. I'm trying to become a vessel for him. This is why I am taking this amazing drug called ZZZZvx ULTRA (XR). It's really enhancing my existence."

Emil did not look up from the magazine. He kept flipping past articles about celebrities who had gotten into some serious trouble.

"That's the craziest shit I've ever heard," said Emil. "This is why you've been acting so fucking weird?"

"Weird? Ha ha ha ha. No, not at all. In fact, I am now more normal than ever since I figured out my life's purpose. ZZZZvx ULTRA (XR) is a Dr. Zweig Altmann drug. It's the surest way possible to maintain peak performance for my man so that way I can one day convince him to fall in love with me."

"That's insane."

"Sorry, what do you mean?"

"I can't do this anymore."

"Emil?"

"No, like, it's too crazy, Reality. You're a really unstable person. You're not yourself. It's, like, you're reading these fucking diplomat magazines from fucking Uzbekistan or whatever the fuck and taking weird-ass designer drugs that are probably just bovine growth hormones and it's making you so gullible that you're going to get yourself sex trafficked or murdered or something worse."

"Emil, I do not understand, nor do I appreciate the lecture. I thought you would be so happy for me now that I'm working hard to become a perfect girlfriend."

"Listen. Like, yes. But also. Like, no. I have to go. I'm sorry. Koffman's chill but this is too weird for me. I'm down for the whole ethereal bimbo with no interiority bit. It's fire. You're fire. Like, I miss being able to hit that. But this is too much. You're on your own."

Emil took the magazine and stuffed it into the back of his B-ball shorts. He walked past the cashiers and did not pay. He just shook his head and rubbed his hands together. And then he was out the door, walking down that strip of Coney Island Avenue that was once our own, that we once walked down together.

As he walked out I thought I heard him say: "Crazy bitch! Fucking cunt! Fucking bitch-ass cunt!"

It was sad about Emil but right now I needed my tribe. Otherwise known as the girlfriends. I had Stefie now. We were in this together, and it was going to be so freaking cool. We had so much to look forward to. We could go to the boutique and pick out nail polish together and sit in the bathroom and paint our toes. I imagined us all on a roller-coaster ride. Maybe we could all play bridge. And when we were together, the main topic of conversation would be our boyfriends, of course. We would all hold hands and talk about our guys' achievements. We would visit Paris, London, and Tokyo. We would have daughters and name them all Rose or Mary Louise.

I could feel my face getting wet. A sign that the ZZZZvx ULTRA (XR) was working. I remember reading the package the first time I picked up the prescription. *Possible Side Effects May Include Deeper Empathy and Therefore Tears.* I certainly was experiencing increased empathy. For the ladies, of course, and for my man, Ariel. As for Emil, he had made his decision and as his friend, I supported him. One fact about being twenty-three is that you learn who your true blues are, and Emil had very conscientiously informed me that he had not made the cut.

It was time to take a walk. I could've gone anywhere, so I decided to go the opposite direction of Emil, south on Coney Island Avenue. The weather was gorgeous and muggy, and outside, as I walked, I saw all of my favorite places. The Laundromat where me and Soo-jin would talk to this one Hasidic woman who was also our age but she had three kids. The gas station where me and Soo-jin used to buy scratch-offs so we could finally become so rich, and Soo-jin could buy an authentic Gucci purse. The Russian banyas where you can eat soup while some mean cunt chases you around with a palm frond and one time me and Soo-jin went together and she screamed "Rape! Rape!" at the man who held the palm frond and we both couldn't stop laughing.

I decided to go into a classic American luncheonette to buy an ice-cold bottle of Coca-Cola to take my mind off of things. I just needed to open the bottle and hear it go "pfahhhhh" and then take a little sip and have all of my worries wash away. Lately all I wanted to drink was Demon NRG X-TREME, but I decided to make an exception, as the luncheonette I had chosen was oh so cute.

The waitress sat me at a blue booth and gave me a menu. I looked around, the lighting was terrible. On the outside, I thought I had found a charming American luncheonette, but inside I saw the place for how it really was: a palace for flies and other vermin! Also, everyone in here was like at least a zillion years old. They probably thought I was some hot stuff! I wondered if they could tell that I had a boyfriend.

Well, I wasn't going anywhere. I was already sitting down. I signaled to the waitress with the help of a few snaps, letting her know I was ready to order.

She looked very tired. She also smelled like a banana.

"I will take a classic and refreshing ice-cold Coca-Cola, please!" I said.

"Anything else?" she asked.

"No, that is all. Ok, thank you!" I responded.

The Coca-Cola was not ice-cold nor was it refreshing and I was feeling really miserable at the luncheonette. Soo-jin was always telling me to drink less ice-cold American Coca-Cola because I had "weak dental hygiene," which was not a true statement but this thought made me have another thought: Was everyone that I knew going to just start lecturing me about my behavior?

I could not think about it right now. I did not appreciate the concern. It is very exhausting to have people comment on your personality. When they are calling you Lil Miss Betrayal Go Fuck Yourself, a migraine will ensue.

I poked around in my tan macramé purse with blue and pink flowers on it and found a few ZZZZvx ULTRA (XR) pills and put them on my tongue and swallowed them with the help of the Coca-Cola. Soon my troubles would be like nothing at all. I'd get the invite that Stefie mentioned. Maybe they would even give me my own crown.

I looked up and the TV was playing. All of the old people were looking at it.

It was another commercial for Adonis-XR.

On the TV, a grandpa-aged man sat on a wood-paneled motorboat next to his gorgeous wife who wore a plastic visor. The motorboat gracefully glided across the turquoise waters of Lake Annecy, passing teenaged kayakers and the occasional lakeside château. The camera zoomed in on the man's face. You now could see that he was smiley and that his teeth were pearly white. Jean Sibelius's "Symphony No. 7" began to play, and the clarinets were the best part. The woman took off her plastic visor and kissed her man on the cheek. He smiled and he put his hand on her bottom, and you could see that she was wearing a tasteful pair of khaki boating shorts.

"Wake up! The future is here. A new era is upon us. Derived from the serene waters of Mount Nothing, Dr. Zweig Altmann's revolutionary Adonis-XR will have you sailing all day—and all night—long," said the soothing voice of an announcer.

It was time to leave. I left a crisp dollar bill on the table, and then walked out. I had places to be. Rumors were swirling about the possibility of a soirée at Paradise that evening. There was always a soirée at Paradise.

SIXTEEN

My intuition was correct. There was going to be a rock 'n' roll show at Paradise that night. All we ever did was a rock 'n' roll show. The stage lights were on, and all of the boys were tuning their instruments and sweeping the floors. The cashbox was out. One of the Joycean Boys sat there counting the currency. I texted all of my new girlfriend friends and invited them to the show and all of them responded with hugs and kisses and said they were all going to obviously be there and were already planning on coming because Ariel was literally so cool and they were just so totally thrilled that I was in their lives ♥♥♥.

I told all of this to Ariel and he seemed pretty surprised that I was going to be at the show that night. "You sure you don't want to do a girls' night or go to an art museum?" he asked when I told him this good news. "One of the boys can do door. You don't have to be here. Derek already got the cashbox out."

"Ha ha ha. No, silly goose! My perfect girls' night is here with my man," I responded, dutifully. Derek was mentally disturbed!

Ariel rolled his eyes and walked away. People were arriving. I took a little bit of the Printesa Sparkle Smell Perfume and sprayed it all over my form. To be a perfect girlfriend is to smell beautiful. Thereby you can support your special guy. I could not wait to once again show the world my man.

When I made my grand entrance, Paradise was full of boyfriends, girlfriends, and various singles. Similar to the Queen, I went up to everyone and gave them the opportunity to kiss my hand. The whole thing was very romantic and classy and I could tell that I was revered by the community at large.

"Reality, darling!!!" said the throngs of patrons. Many of them asked me where they could possibly find my signature scent. I informed them that a lady never reveals her secrets. I sauntered over to the door, where the same Joycean Boy, Derek, was counting bills.

"Money problems?" I said to the boy. "Tell me about it. The Dow Jones and the S&P 500 are not looking good, according to the top papers about financial well-being."

The Joycean Boy, Derek, continued to count his cash.

"Ha ha," he responded. "Want to do a key bump of some ketamine?"

Naturally, I obliged the gentleman and gladly snorted as he took his ketamine covered key and put it beneath my nostril.

Ketamine! I felt pretty awesome. I thanked the boy and did a curtsy, so he knew that I respected his authority greatly. The line at the door was sizable, which I was super glad about. Everyone was wearing their evening finery. They all stood there dressed in the outfits of various courtiers. I waved and informed them that it would just be a moment and then the music would begin.

I couldn't wait until the girlfriends arrived. They were going to have such a fabulous time this evening. It was going to be awesome. The lineup was stacked and I was looking pretty beautiful myself. I was a perfect hostess.

HOW TO BE A PERFECT HOSTESS

What's on the menu today, ladies? Perhaps it is duck confit, deviled eggs, an aspic. And you will go to the shopping center for flowers. The marketplace will have just what you need for entertaining. Put the peonies in a trumpet vase with a little bit of water. While the food is cooking, you are going to put your hair in some hot rollers and begin to get ready for your evening of entertainment. A champagne cocktail is a must-have. Your guests are going to be delighted by the French 75.

When they arrive you will be wearing your apron and your hair is now perfectly coiffed. "We are charmed," the guests will say when they see your fine display. Several of your guests are international politicians and some are doctors of philosophy. Congratulations: you are now a world-class hostess and your boyfriend knows this as well so tonight you will be rewarded by hugs and kisses.

Everything was simply going swimmingly. The guests were standing around the stage. The band was about to start. The girlfriends were about to be fashionably late. Derek was counting his money. I peeked out the door. It was Medhi! What a delight it would be to have the sculptor Medhi at the show.

"Ah," said Medhi. "It is you. La jeune américaine. Très bien. Can you to please tell your boyfriend he is going to be quiet now?"

"Medhi," I responded. "We are having dignified guests over tonight for an evening of fine music. We would absolutely love to have you."

"It is impossible to do my art project when the Unabomber is having post-punk concerts upstairs!" said Medhi.

I smiled. This was going to be difficult. Remembering my hostess skills, I quickly fashioned Medhi a champagne cocktail. French 75, made from a Joycean Boy's stash of various alcohols purchased for convivial events.

"Bon?" I said.

Medhi swatted the drink away with disgust. "It is very bad!"

I was growing frustrated. The man could not be assuaged!

I took a deep breath and fluttered my eyelids to maintain a level of class and poise. He was gone.

Girlfriends . . . vanilla, jasmine, rose, cedarwood—flowers of romance. Dresses of Swiss dot, chiffon, satin. Strappy high-heeled sandals in gold. The beautiful girls have arrived! And oh, I was charmed, so positively charmed to see them. Stefie, Mallory, the whole gang was here to support my boyfriend Ariel's special night of music. As they walked in, they kissed me on the cheek and Derek said, "Five dollars," and I told him to seriously shut the fuck up these were VIP guests.

I got the girlfriends French 75s and offered them raspberry dark chocolate truffles from a box that said вкусный шоколад. They smiled and thanked me and I grabbed their mink stoles and the whole thing made my heart pitter-patter. The girlfriends made themselves at home. They whipped out their smokes and sat down on the couches and had a really nice time. They touched each other's hair and took drags of one another's cigarettes and I could tell that my girls had my back and that they were going to be so proud of me for such a festive and well-attended event.

The first band was on and I couldn't figure out what their deal was. I suppose it was krautrock inspired? What I mean by this is each of their songs was fifteen minutes long and it was all made up of these super proggy drones. It was all boys on the stage. Boyfriends, by the looks of it. They just stood there, hunched over their instruments wearing Hawaiian shirts and the frontman mumbled stuff into the microphone but it was impossible to understand what he was saying. The audience wasn't really paying attention. Everyone was looking at their feet, or they were kissing, or they were enjoying the champagne cocktails. I suppose it was up to the guests to spend the evening however they liked, yet I could feel myself getting flustered because as the hostess, you would think everyone would sit silently and enjoy the beautiful sounds of rock 'n' roll even if the band was indebted to the krautrock style! I poured a little gin in my champagne flute so therefore I'd be calm.

I could hear whispering and it was preventing me from having a fully immersive experience. I was moving and grooving and it was very frustrating for someone to cramp my style in this way. I turned around.

To my surprise, what I saw was the girlfriends. They were doing their siren speak. I suppose I should've known it was them. They were speaking in such glamorous and hushed tones. It was not so obvious as to what I was supposed to do. It was important for me to continue to seem like I was approachable and calm, so I was leaning toward not saying anything. But maybe being just a tad bit assertive was exactly what I needed to do! I remember learning this at eight years old: if you are kind and use good manners you may tell someone, hey, no, stop that I do not like that! Perhaps this was the correct method. Or maybe it was somewhere in between. Make it seem like no biggie, tee-hee-hee. I could say: "Ohh miii God it's literally no worries at all ahahhahah. I'm actually just, like, super trying to enjoy this band that is indebted to the krautrock style! But, like, totally feel free to keep talking! I'm actually super relaxed!"

I looked at the girlfriends and they looked at me. "It's awesome that you guys are having some chitchat! You girls are awesome," I said. The girlfriends, the beautiful sirens. Those bodacious babes. They looked at me and said: "Ha ha. Yeah."

Then I turned around and saw Soo-jin.

I did not know who invited her to this place. To be honest, me and Soo-jin had not been speaking lately because she didn't support my lifestyle choices. But here she was, at Paradise, next to all of the beautiful girlfriends. Soo-jin looked very different from my new friends. This was not a glamorous individual. This was not a lady-in-waiting. This was someone dressed in the costume of the girls who attended our college. Terra-cotta-colored pants that you will wear if you are a construction worker, lesbian, or your habitat is an apartment near a popular graveyard and you have two roommates. A white blouse which is to be worn while sipping your tea in the French countryside c. 1915 (the wind is a permanent fixture, coming off of the bluffs). Hair in two greasy braids and many, many earrings on the ears.

I found her appearance to be disquieting because Soo-jin technically *was* a girlfriend. She was always saying to me: "Lord Byron is the love of my life." She was always walking around my former residence in the nude eating applesauce out of a clear plastic bag while Lord Byron took calls on the couch. When I asked her about it she would say: "You wouldn't get it, when you're that comfortable around someone, you could wear a bandana as pants and they'd still want to jump your bones." Then some applesauce would drip onto her boob.

Neither of us said anything to each other.

Then she introduced herself to Stefie, who was currently fanning herself with a fan.

"Hey," she said. "Nice fan."

"Ew, a homeless person!" said Stefie.

"I'm Reality's best friend," she said.

SEVENTEEN

We went up to the roof and sat down on an inflatable couch. From up here, I could still kind of make out the band that was indebted to the krautrock style. From up here, I felt like a real girl in New York City. I could see everything. In the distance: the ocean, the train, a single church, the clocktower, this one building where I knew that deals were occurring probably this very instant. I briefly allowed myself time to imagine life as the girlfriend of a financier instead of Ariel. I briefly allowed myself to forget Soo-jin was there, too. I just wanted to feel like a lady of the city. She holds a rose and stands backlit by a skylight. She walks barefoot on a velvet carpet. They are always holding a door open for her. The driver wears a black cap, with a golden trim. She takes her meals on the terrace.

I think this was a moment where I had been very silent for longer than usual. I looked at Soo-jin. She had a look on her face that said: I am really sad about something. I did not know what the look on my face was, but here was what I was experiencing in my heart: a heaving kind of feeling. I did not enjoy having this experience in my heart. I wished it would go away, like a red-tailed hawk with sacred information who must make its peregrinations across land and sea.

"So this is where you've been spending all your time the past few months," she said, finally. "That girl downstairs was mean."

"That's my friend Stefie, she is a very respected member of my friend group, which you are not in," I said in response.

"Ok, Reality," said Soo-jin. "Can you be serious for like five minutes, please."

"No one invited you to this party! If you do not wish to respect the girlfriends, who have helped me find my true purpose in life, which is being a girlfriend, you are welcome to leave."

"Jesus Christ," she said. "You invited me here, Reality. You texted me and told me to come."

"I did not do this."

"Ok, you know what. I am so exhausted. I know you're feeling something right now. I can tell because you are doing that thing you do where you squint your eyes and look out at the horizon line and start tapping your foot."

I stopped squinting my eyes and looking out at the horizon line as well as tapping my foot.

"Do you remember when we were in college, when we stayed up all night on amphetamines on the last day of finals and went swimming in the wastewater treatment plant. And Lord Byron did a cannonball and you did a starfish float."

"Yes, the past can be used to color a girlfriend's life so she seems approachable and interesting to her boyfriend."

There was another pause of silence, and the image of the terrace reentered my brain.

"I loved you in college. You were always wearing skorts and shaving different parts of your head. You listened to music on a Walkman even though no one did that anymore. Everyone thought you were a genius," said Soo-jin. "Ok, you know what, I'm just going to read this thing I wrote down on my cell phone."

Soo-jin pulled out her cell phone and began to read.

Dear Reality,

It's your friend Soo-jin.

Are we even friends? At one point I was your best friend.

And now you treat me like nothing.

Because you finally have a boyfriend for the first time in your life.

It's not that interesting to be regularly fucking someone.

Having a boyfriend isn't an identity.

It's a totally normal thing to do.

I know I sound like a hypocrite because I already met the love of my life.

But it's true. It's not that interesting.

And Ariel? I honestly do not get it. Just because someone goes to graduate school doesn't mean they're smart.

Let me know when you're ready to be my friend again. Honestly I don't know if I want to be your friend again.

Let me know when you're ready to grow up.

EIGHTEEN

That was awkward. After Soo-jin read her speech, I knew I had to get away from her. I was aware that being the greatest girlfriend involves being tested, but I did not appreciate this. I needed to find Ariel. Where was Ariel? I needed a cigarette. It was time to find a cigarette.

I slinked around the roof, doing an air guitar with my hands and taking my fingers and pretending they were pistols at high noon. Someone needed to have a cigarette for me. I was really fiending for one. I knew it was not exactly ladylike, but Stefie was always ripping cigs, so I assumed it couldn't be such a big deal to have one at a cultural event such as this one.

Ariel . . . I could smell him. And I could hear him! I knew that he occasionally had an evening smoke, so it was likely that he could furnish me with a cigarette of my own. Using my houndly intuition for figuring out where my owner was, I found Ariel. He was all the way on the other side of the roof with his friend Katie. Ariel had his hand on her back, and they were both smoking some crack. He was laughing. Katie was telling jokes and gesticulating the way you do when you are in true love. They seemed like they were having a really nice time in each other's company. Suddenly I was not feeling so good. Suddenly I remembered the important lesson I had learned. Suddenly I was fantasizing about a painful and fiery death by way of the Turkmenistan Darvaza Gas Crater, "Door to Hell." I decided to walk up to them and chugged the remaining gin in my champagne flute. As I approached, I could see that sweetie pie baby moved his hand up to Katie's neck. He was rubbing it.

"Ariel!" I said.

"Oh," said Ariel.

"It's great to see you, darling! Are you pounding Katie's pussy? PS, can I have a cigarette! I am fiending for a smoke. Thanks so much, you are special to me!"

"Reality," said Ariel. "You're wasted."

"Actually, I've only had, like, six champagne cocktails and some gin, plus some ketamine and anyways, you know that I am an idiosyncratic character who tends to speak her mind! At least I'm not serenely smoking crack cocaine. A cigarette will do!"

Neither Ariel nor Katie responded. They both looked at me and passed the crack pipe between each other.

"What are you talking about?" said Ariel, finally. "Let me call you a car."

"I will not need this! It's no biggie if you're pounding Katie's pussy. I remain chaste for you. Thanks to the lesson you taught me, my heart and body will remain open for you at all times."

"Hey," said Katie. "Ariel said you've had a hard week, but you're being disruptive."

"Reality," said Ariel. "I'm so tired of this."

I blinked. I didn't want to ruin the vibe so I went back downstairs to the girlfriends.

It was in between sets now so the girlfriends were all sitting around having a great time. They were laughing and they had their legs crossed. I wasn't sure what was going on with Ariel, but I knew that I was still a girlfriend so everything was totally chill and all good. I bet the girlies were really excited for the next act and then were going to do something really fabulous afterward like have hamburgers and martinis at a classic French bistro where the tablecloths are checkered and the waiters wear all white.

"It's seriously so crazy that before I moved to NYC I had never ever even tasted an avocado before," said a girlfriend with feathery porn star hair. I was pretty sure her name was Delia and that she was the girlfriend of Eduardo, the real estate agent of Ariel's friend group. "Just imagine, you start your freshman year at fashion school and you've never even tasted an avocado before! Eduardo thought it was so funny."

The girlfriends all started to giggle. I loved to be a fly on the wall for such merry chatter. "Your boyfriend is, like, totally a slumlord, Delia." Mallory laughed. "Ok, let's go! Let's go. On y va les filles."

"Tu parles français aussi?" I said, as I approached the girlfriends.

"Ahaha bah oui," said Mallory. "Je suis Suisse en fait."

En fait, I didn't know that Mallory was Suisse.

I noticed that the next band was starting. They were less krauty than the opener, but I still enjoyed their oblique and atonal approach to song.

"C'est sympa!" I responded. "Ok, alors, vous êtes en train de partir? C'est dommage!"

Mallory looked at me and patted my ass. "It's cute that you can speak French. Guys like it when you can speak a second language. Everyone will love your whole vibe once you get the invite."

I looked up at the band again. It was certainly jangle rock time! "That's awesome even though I don't totally know what you mean by invite! Anyways, as I was saying in the French language earlier, are you leaving? It's such an amazing evening of music and I wouldn't want you girls to miss it!"

Mallory and the girlfriends whispered among themselves for a moment. In the meantime, I started picking at a cut on my hand and it obviously started gushing blood immediately. "We're totally leaving, sorry, girlfriend! But come with us," said Mallory.

Considering that I was pretty sure that my boyfriend, Ariel, was porking Katie, I decided to go on a journey into the milky night with the girlfriends. I had to admit, I was pretty excited. It seemed reckless to leave in the middle of a show at Paradise but I was sure the Joycean Boys would manage.

Also, I never did anything bad. That was one of the main facts about Reality. I was fundamentally someone who only bent the rules when it came to doing Serbian research chemicals or making kind of an interesting zine. Besides that, I was a really normal girl who appreciated order and structure. I really needed to let loose more! And also I know I was supposed to be submissive for my man at all times but there was something inside of me that seemed to say: *No, abandon Ariel, who is maybe not the boyfriend.*

NINETEEN

Oh! We moved with such elegant velocity. We were like a divine girl centipede, snaking its way through the streets, bombarding the general public with our fit and flare frocks, our skirt suit sets, our dresses of fine materials such as organdy and chiffon. Us girlfriends—in our makeup, with our hair so perfect, with our nails so perfectly manicured—we were a gorgeous sight to behold. It was eyes on us as we drank our Evan Williams in a highball glass. It was girlfriend time as we fingered our pool cues. It was Girlfriend City as we hailed taxicabs and giggled and let our hands linger over our sensitive parts. I could feel a new kind of love coursing through my veins, and I couldn't tell if it was because I was on a heroic dose of ZZZZvx ULTRA (XR) or if it was because I was simply experiencing a brand-new form of sisterhood and it was so very nice.

We were at one of those dancing clubs where what you do is drink a martini dry, ice-cold glass, and everyone is wearing something black and leathery and the walls are all mirrors and the music is disco balls, hi-hats, sparkle synthesizer. It was one, two, three martinis, dry, ice-cold, and so I went to the bathroom and sat in the stall and counted the number of drinks I had consumed that evening. One, two, three, four, five, six, seven, eight. I was feeling pretty drunk so I went back to dancing and Stefie took my waist and pressed it to her pelvis and in the mirrors we could see our reflections. Everything was good and I was at the apex of my confidence. I pursed my lips together and rolled my eyes back so I was in seizure mode. I was hardly in Stefie's arms for five minutes—oh, if Ariel could see! I didn't even care about what he was up to right now. I was with my girlfriends. I was committing a criminal act, sneaking off like this—it was a period where crimes were de rigueur.

Then the music changed—it was no longer disco balls, it was tropicália. Us girlfriends were all babes in arms. We flexed our arms and shook our hips. A piano which was dissonant began to play and then it was congas and cackling that was so loud it made my whole body vibrate.

This was what I was meant to be doing. I felt this with every fiber of Reality's being. It was true that I was destined for evenings dancing like this. I was so happy, happy, happy to really move my body. I was feeling thrilled on the account of the fact that I had finally found a group. I could feel a pressure building up inside of me and suddenly I was very warm. I was so hot in my outfit. I had an urge to be naked. I wished that I could speak Portuguese. I was feeling really angry that I was not living in the São Paulo of the sixties. I wished to urgently be wearing nothing but my espadrilles and to be lying out by the turquoise sea.

And one day I would be. I had this feeling that a lot of things were about to change for me, big time. I was destined for the stage. I was destined to be the perfect girlfriend. I just had to make a few adjustments and I would be Ariel's perfect little girl. It came to me easily and perfectly: there would be an invite. Yes, I was on my way to being so very lucky. My problems would simply melt away once I was given the opportunity to better myself for the good of the community.

Stefie Stefana Stef. She grabbed my hand and as I followed her it was like I was the tail of a comet, viewable in the deep dark blue sky. She grabbed my chin. Oh, it was the feeling of heaven. "You're going to go to Mount Nothing soon, I can tell," she said breathlessly. Why was Stefie telling me this now? Was she also in a girlfriend-induced state of reverie? "You're going to get the invite soon. I haven't been yet. I haven't gotten the invite yet mostly because of my internship. But you will because you're a perfect girlfriend. You're passing all of the ultimate tests with flying colors. Seriously. I mean, look at you," said Stefie, taking her hand and moving it across my body. "Really good stuff. Ugh."

"Stefie," I said. "It doesn't even matter. I'm pretty sure that Ariel and Katie are having sex again and I am concerned this is my fault. Perhaps

I was not dedicated enough and did not have a wet enough pussy for my special guy when he was teaching me his important lesson."

"Reality," said Stefie. "You're doing an amazing job. Seriously. You're so good at being a girlfriend. Sometimes our special guys have to go off to the war and you just have to support them and give them love and maybe go on a special trip so you can come back and really be perfect."

WHAT TO DO WHEN YOUR BOYFRIEND
IS OFF FIGHTING IN THE WARS

Ciao, girlfriends. Yes, frequently it is happening that your man he is fighting in wars. For example, the religious crusades or World War II or Iraq. Having a boyfriend who is in the army is considered noble and for this you may wear a ribbon made of fine silk. Perhaps a dinner party is in order, yet you must explain for what reason Adam is not to be joining the meal tonight. "He is fighting the war," you say to the guests. "It is impressive that he is off doing service abroad in the war," they respond. "And next it is the aspic we will be eating," you tell the guests. Then they all clap because it is impressive to have a boyfriend who fights in the war and also that you are quite the little chef de cuisine!

I went back to Paradise and it was pretty empty. There was music playing but there were only a few people around. They were just having some beverages. I thought about making some pleasant discussion. One of the things I had learned recently is that a good hostess does her job until the last drop has been consumed. At this time of night, the guests should be offered the final digestif and their drivers have been phoned or the valet will return their Rolls-Royces. Additionally, if your boyfriend is not present you can say he is fighting in the war.

I really did want to be a good hostess. I wanted everyone to know that they were seen! And also welcome in the space. I thought about opening up a bottle of amaro, yet I found myself swimming in sadness, so I went to Ariel's room and took out my coloring equipment to make my zine.

I drew a picture. It was of me (Reality), wearing one of my customary beautiful dresses. In the picture, I was wearing a tiara and my hair was a crazy rainbow and I had on Lucite slippers. Next to me was my boyfriend, Ariel. We were holding hands. Also, in the background you can see a rock 'n' roll band. Since this is a picture of some of my favorite things I imagined that the band was playing music indebted to the krautrock style!

I sat there and kept working. I did some writing. I wrote all about Paradise and the things you could do there. I included facts about the Joycean Boys and picked out a few quotes from *Ulysses* that I was simply hearing all the time.

I also included some facts about me and Ariel and our true love and how even though he was being distant, by maybe sleeping with Katie again, I wasn't even mad because I was seriously in love with him. I started to feel buzzy and warm all over again. This was probably because I had consumed so many alcoholic beverages, but I think it was also because making my art is known to put me in a really great mood. The world was really coming into focus for me right now. Everything was feeling really bright and sharp, like I was wearing a pair of extra-useful glasses that maybe have infrared, or like I was a dog who could predict the rain.

In a lot of ways, my life was really good. Basically, I was gorgeous, and I had made new friends. I was especially enamored by Stefie. I also couldn't help but think about the invite and how I would be receiving this shortly. I knew that whatever it involved, it was certainly going to help me show Ariel that I was number one. That I was one of the most elite girlfriends in the whole world. Not everyone got the invite. Special girls got the invite. If you were a really good hostess, you got the invite.

you love a
certain person

— joyce

My host duties! I had only meant to spend just a few minutes making my radical art document to be consumed by the children of the future. It really was time to make sure that the final guests felt appropriately taken care of in their remaining time at Paradise (#221). It was my duty to ensure it. Well, mine and also my assistants. Where were the Joycean Boys after all? Where were my dudes-in-waiting? Where was the idiot who counted the money? Where was the one who kept telling me facts about the philosophy of Jean François Lyotard? I seriously wished I had a gun or something so I could threaten those wretched boys. They were idiots and needed to learn a thing or two about the art of being a host.

I stomped around and couldn't find them anywhere. I yelled out their names and none of them responded. I went to each of the shipping containers and said: "Open the fuck up I have a literal fucking gun," and to my dismay this useful tactic yielded no boys. I went into the bathroom and they weren't there, either. Had they left? This was impossible. This is what I got for letting those idiot boys run the place while I had a beautiful reverie with the girlfriends.

I decided to just pretend it wasn't a big deal and offer the remaining guests some of the amaro I had purchased and then tell them their patronage was much appreciated. They said: Wait, who are you? And so I said: I'm Ariel's girlfriend. You can also call me the Bitch of Paradise.

AND NOW FOR A SECOND INTERMISSION,

COURTESY OF THE GIRLFRIEND WEEKLY

CORPORATION OF HOW YOU MAKE THE

BEAUTIFUL WOMAN TO BE GLAMOROUS, YES!!!!!

HOW TO EMBRACE THE SPIRITUAL SO THAT
IT WILL BE TRUE LOVE FOREVER

We have now reached the Azores, an autonomous archipelago off the coast of Portugal (ha ha ha say that five times fast: the Azores, an autonomous archipelago; the Azores, an autonomous archipelago; the Azores, an autonomous archipelago; the Azores, an autonomous archipelago; the Azores, an autonomous archipelago).

Girlfriends, hello! We love you and respect your journeys. It is certain that you are looking for a spiritual guide to help you achieve true love forever. If you have not yet visited the temple of Angkor Wat, this is considered to be helpful to find the true path. You could also visit the city of Petra. Do you even know where Babylon is on a map? The Assyrians were a decadent culture and in the end their licentiousness could not save them. This magazine has been used for one thousand years as counsel. If your name is Valerie Estelle Kahn you have a boyfriend named Ariel Koffman who has the charm of the surfer Miki Dora and is a former child genius of the piano. Do you remember Hadrian? Latin is considered a dead language now. Sed omnia praeclara tam difficilia quam rara sunt. But you can still hear it in the church. Well, not as much as in the wow and flutter before the Concilium Oecumenicum Vaticanum Secundum. It was heaven back then. Oh, to be Jeanne D'Arc as the flames rose to her Semitic nose and her Walkman started to melt. What am I? Aquilinus of Davyhulme? To become religious is as simple as taking ZZZZvx ULTRA (XXR) and telling Dr. Altmann, thank you, thank you!

VOLUME FOUR

GIRLFRIEND

When they had been dating for one year the girl sighed like a baby bird. *Imagine now that the wings are fluttering.* The girl couldn't wait to see what the boy had planned for their special day, their one-year anniversary. *Imagine now that in a nightmare scenario the boy says, Oh shit, sorry, did you actually want to do something together? I'm kind of busy tonight.* Her eyes welled with tears. *Imagine now that she remembered something about Geneva—a one-way plane ticket, an invite.* She told him it was no worries at all. She actually had to do something. She had to go on a trip. *Imagine now that all of your problems could be solved if you went to a place called Mount Nothing. Imagine that all of your dreams were about to come true—provided that you do a good job.*

At that moment, now boarding the plane, she realized she was so scared. She was so scared. It was so scary.

Here is why she was scared. Here is why it was so scary: because sometimes you love someone so much and you know, you know, you just know they do not love you back. And what the fuck do you do then?

That she would be scared was decided from the moment she had been bornth. Because when a baby is bornth she is scared to be alive. She wants to go back inside. No cowboy in a powder blue suit could be her protector. And it was all her new best friends in the place they call Mount Nothing that reminded her of this fact. All of her new friends in the place that they call Mount Nothing who had picked her up from the Geneva airport in an unmarked white Sprinter van. They reminded her that when you are scared you want to go back inside. And there were even more new friends waiting for her when the unmarked Sprinter van made its final destination. They were all waiting there on that sandy coast of Lake Annecy 2, which is a lake that looks just like Lake Annecy only it is different for a variety of reasons. There were hundreds of them waiting on that sandy coast. Hundreds of girlfriends with boyfriends. Boyfriends who they fucked and sucked and lay there and took it. Boyfriends who had taught them lessons. Boyfriends who they would do anything for.

And they were all dressed in white, the girlfriends. And they all had kindly facial expressions and comely features. And they all were holding flowers. And when they took a razor and shaved the girl's head they giggled. And they all cleaned up the vomit from the girl's face when she finally stopped retching. And they all gave a soprano sigh when the girl said, *What is happening to me? I didn't ask for this.* They all patted her on her back, told her that in just a little bit she would fall asleep and have very pleasant dreams. They all told her that her new name was Girlfriend. Because that's who they all were: girlfriends. And when you come here, to Mount Nothing, which is the main mountain at Lake Annecy 2, you get the chance to prove yourself. You get the chance to prove that you are the greatest girlfriend of all time. You get a fresh start. A chance to make things right. A chance to see your quest to its natural conclusion.

So let's follow Girlfriend on her quest. Let's follow her and see her quest to its natural conclusion.

Read on, *man.*

IN WHICH REALITY GOES TO MOUNT NOTHING

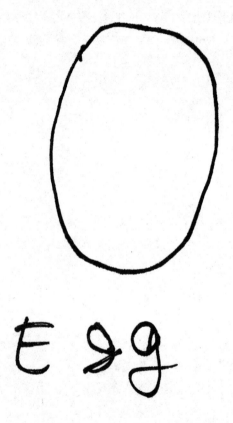

Egg

INTAKE

This was a peculiar time. My name was now Girlfriend and I was in a room of hundreds just like me, sitting in little plastic chairs, wearing white dresses, bald on the head. I did not know how I got here from the airport. I was acting like a child with an affliction. I was aware that there had been violence done to my form. And a feeling of terror remained. But I was certain that the future would show itself if I followed the rules and did what I was told. Because when you are experiencing the feeling of terror, that could be because you will have a new and exciting experience.

This new and exciting experience happened because of the invite that I had received. It was a voice on the telephone. Toll-free, of course. It was a one-way ticket to Geneva. It was a feeling of weightlessness at a transatlantic thirty thousand feet. Of sipping on the intoxicant Jim Beam and sucking down the famous pills. It was all very exciting. And now the girlfriends. Yes, the girlfriends. That is who we all were. We were all here together in this room with picture windows where you can see the sparkling blue waters, the tennis courts, the waterslides. I took a deep breath. I smiled. This felt right. I was safe among all these girlfriends, ensconced in this little egg of a room.

I saw a desk. And at the desk what I heard was *clack clack clack*. Were more girlfriends there? Several. This was a girlfriend typing pool, by the sound of it. I wondered what it was they were typing. I bet they were looking at websites, blinking at them. Making deals. Perhaps they had accessed the part of the Internet where you can buy an assault rifle similar to the one Soo-jin said Ariel should own or a child servant or some strappy high-heeled shoes.

I decided to walk up. To do this, I put one foot in front of the other. My balance felt off, I wasn't really sure why. I was feeling very wobbly. I was worried I'd trip. It was possible that I would trip and eat shit. Using my training from being a girlfriend who went on long walks on the beach, I put my hands on my hips and directed my gaze directly at the desk.

When I arrived at the desk it was three girlfriends. They had beautiful bald heads and beautiful blue eyes. Basically they were triplets. Only distinct in their choice of dress. "We're processing your travel documents as well as your letter of intent to be one of the greatest girlfriends of all time," said a girlfriend in a white turtleneck and white wool pants. "Please, if you would tell us the date of your first dose."

I stroked my chin just like my friend Emil. I giggled. I readjusted my bosom. I opened my heart. I thought long and hard about the details. That first day felt so long ago. I suppose it had been a year? Had it been so long since I became Ariel's? I told them this. I said in my best, sweetest, happiest, and most grateful voice, my answer. I had been Ariel's for twelve months. And I had been on ZZZZvx ULTRA (XR) for nine. No major side effects. I was more beautiful than ever, even though I now had no head hair. Happy all the time. Grateful for my boyfriend. Always lubricated for intercourse. Even when asleep. Sense of purpose. This is the biggest change. I know exactly why I was bornth.

The girlfriend in the white turtleneck kept typing, nodding her head. "Thank you," she said. "Open up your mouth." I did just this and she placed a pill on my tongue. "A little ZZZZvx ULTRA (XXR) for the road! Now feel free to return to your seat. It will just be a moment, gorgeous. And do let us know at any point during your onboarding with us if you experience any negative side effects from your new dose of Dr. Altmann's drug. Symptoms to look out for are migraine headaches, diarrhea, evil thoughts, suicidal thoughts, forbidden thoughts, and thoughts of breaking up with your special guy."

Of course. The girlfriends had my best interests at heart. It was comforting to know that if I developed evil thoughts or diarrhea, the lovely ladies would come to my rescue. To the tune of the girlfriends clicking their mouses and typing on their keyboards I Skipped-to-My-Lou back to my little chair, next to a girlfriend wearing some sunglasses called aviator. Just a moment now. Soon I would begin the next phase of onboarding. I was sure everything would all be explained so soon. For now, I had the joy of looking at the lake called Lake Annecy 2. This beautiful lake. I tried hard to think of a happy memory, any happy memory, but when I closed my eyes, all I saw was the word *Ariel*, lit up in neon, twirling around as if on a plate. *Ariel, Ariel, Ariel.*

Then the door opened.

THUS SPOKE ARIEL

MALL

The Atlantic Terminal Mall 2 was one of my all-time favorite spots. I suppose it had been a while since I'd been there, since I had been to the mall which is in a field of lupines at sunset in a place they call Mount Nothing. Girlfriends: there were hundreds of them here, going into the stores, eating fried chicken, trying on a hat at a dastardly place called Lids. The terror of Lids was feeling really palpable at this moment.

Ariel was here, too, wearing his headphones and holding the ancient device called Walkman.

"Oh hey, Girlfriend!" he said. "It's me, Ariel! Nice bald head. Sorry I've been so distant recently. It's because I've been doing a lot of thinking. You have no idea how stressful it is to be turning twenty-seven so soon. That's when life starts to matter! I know I missed our one-year anniversary last week, that wasn't chill of me and I want to make it up to you. That's why I'm here, at the Atlantic Terminal Mall 2 in this field of lupines."

"Ariel," I responded. Where were the rest of my words? It was as if I could hardly speak.

"Ok, I'll tell you how I'm going to make it up to you. If you do a good job following me around and doing various tasks, maybe things will work out between us and I'll stop being so stressed about turning twenty-seven years old. All you have to do is be the greatest girlfriend ever, don't think too hard about it."

We walked onto the escalator. Ariel grabbed my hand. "Wow," he said, looking upon the vaulted ceiling and the fountain down below. "These grounds certainly are not fallow."

I wanted to say that I agreed, and that if I had an ample dowry, he would be impressed, and, in fact, would inherit dozens of serfs called "Reality's Kids." But I still could not form words other than "Ariel," and "Oh," and "Huh," so I just fixed my gaze upon his visage and hoped this was the right thing to do.

When we reached the bottom, Ariel instructed me to do acrobatics, such as a handstand, a backbend, a split, and a somersault. He told me to go into the wretched store Lids and cartwheel around like a wee babe. I was not a gymnast, this was not one of my skills as a girlfriend, so I had to try my best. And this was especially difficult because there were no gymnast mats in case of falling.

"Oof, not so good, Girlfriend," said Ariel. "You're pretty bad at doing acrobatics here in the Atlantic Terminal Mall 2. I'm not sure you have what it takes, but we will continue on."

BALLET

The theater had red velvet curtains and a small stage and the lighting was one lamp on the floor from a place called Ikea. Ariel had informed me we would be doing a dance called Daphnis et Chloé by Maurice Ravel, and this was considered expert level and we would be partnered with a third dancer named Katie who had a green mullet and an awesome vibe. I did not have experience as a ballerina. This was not like acting in a play, which was one of my skills.

I had to think on my feet. They gave me a pair of pale pink ballet slippers to aid me with this taxing trial. The curtains opened. The girlfriends were all in the audience eating popcorn and cheering. First it was a harp, then the caw of the horns and a first violin that screamed like it was coming out of the moss. And I, Chloé, fainted so perfectly into the arms of the beloved, the beloved who is Ariel but also Daphnis. And it began to snow. The snow was a real snow. And Daphnis grabbed my waist, tossed me up in the air. An oboe. The strings crescendoed, bursting and blooming. And the third dancer, Katie, who played the role of the nymph, danced around him. Around Daphnis. And inside my heart everything tightened. And the nymph jumped, did a plié. Katie Katie Katie. Through her movements, we learn the story of when she met Ariel. It was when he and his college girlfriend were on a break, you see. They were in an open relationship. Ariel and Urbi were on a break. A long love, it was a long love. Four years—a whole lifetime when you are age twenty-two. The nymph enters the arms of Daphnis. And I, Chloé, realized that there is water on my face. I was weeping.

"Not very becoming of the greatest girlfriend of all time!" a girlfriend shouts from the audience.

TRUE LOVE, PT. I

To be the greatest girlfriend of all time, you have to be able to tell a story. So this is what I did.

A rural route, soft yellowish headlights cutting through the fog. The car drives past a swath of pine trees, past the Great Meat Store of the North, past the firewood store, past the fleuve Hudson and its fabulous gorge (oh how it was deep, oh how it swirled). This is a place of great significance for the girl, age twenty-three. Here, the skating over frozen ponds. Here, the School Street VFW. Here, smoking a bong in the basement of a gay guy, her best friend. Here, the girl named Kansas, a violent streak of pink light born from the cradle of the void, the swapping of spit featuring tongue. Here, the army base with its warplanes of great destruction, their flight paths, a bottle rocket pointed to the sky. Here, the loving mother and the loving father, sitting at the enamel dining room table.

She was young here once. Younger than age twenty-three, which some say is the youngest age a person can be. *2006 Honda Accord, Gala Apple Red.* She puts the car in park. The boy, age twenty-six, wakes up, startled. He grabs her hand. They walk inside. The girl pours him a scotch, neat. The good stuff from her parents. The boy takes a sip and walks around.

"It's really weird," says the boy. "That all of these fridge magnets and awards say *Valerie*, not *Reality*."

The girl says nothing. There is something about how she can't really talk. She picks at her crotch. She is known to do just this.

The boy gulps down the scotch. He picks up a picture of the girl. She is age seven, in a calico dress her grammy got for her on a work trip to London. She is age seven, in a pair of saddle shoes. She is age seven, missing her two front teeth. She is age seven, holding hands with a cowboy in a powder blue suit. The boy does not know it but the photograph was taken in Hollywood, Florida. He does not know about skating on frozen ponds. He does not know about the gay guy and his bong. He scratches his nose. He is known to do just this.

"Sometimes," he says, "I feel like you have no opinions about anything. Like, you're afraid to tell me what you're thinking because you're scared something bad will happen. You're so fucking agreeable it makes my skin crawl. I'm literally begging you to have literally any ownership of your thoughts. I'm literally begging you to say literally anything."

The girl continues to say nothing. The boy walks over to her and touches her boob.

"I guess it doesn't matter, Valerie, *Val.*" He laughs, rubbing her left nipple. "Realistically, this is the last time I'll be here."

The girl continues to say nothing. The boy makes a gesture as if to say, *Let's fuck.*

BEDTIME

One of the skills the greatest girlfriend of all time must possess is to lay there and take it. So when I was brought to the bedroom in the style of Louis XV and the music started to play, I knew what to do. But this time it was not jazz or classical, it was something they call EDM. And it was so loud. The music was so loud. And the lights began to strobe. And I felt drunk on alcohol and drool pooled out of my mouth and my eye twitched. And I felt drunk on alcohol, so I slumped over and hit my head and there was some blood on my forehead. And when Ariel walked into the room he told me that when you are in Mount Nothing you have the opportunity to teach your girlfriend a lesson. And when Ariel put me up on the bed he took off my shoes and my panties but not my dress, so I closed my eyes and he covered my mouth and I felt the blood getting hotter and running faster and he whispered in my ear that I was so drunk, it's so cute, that he really loved to fuck me and in my brain I pictured what a pink Jeep under the Manhattan Bridge would look like if someone threw a car bomb at it. I said nothing I did not tell him that it hurt that it hurt that it hurt and so I just clenched my teeth and I lay there and I take it and when it is over I am told I have finally done something right for once and when it is done I smile big and I try hard to think of a happy memory, any happy memory, but when I closed my eyes, all I saw was the word *Ariel*, lit up in neon, twirling around as if on a plate. *Ariel, Ariel, Ariel.*

TRUE LOVE, PT. 2

To be the greatest girlfriend of all time, you have to be able to tell a story. So this is what I did.

Here is, at this moment, what *Reality* (not Valerie or *Val*) is thinking:

I love you I love you I love you I love you I love you I love you I love you
I love you I love you I love you I love you I love you I love you I love you
I love you I love you I love you I love you I love you I love you I love you
I love you I love you I love you I love you I love you I love you I love you
I love you I love you I love you I love you I love you I love you I love you
I love you I love you I love you I love you I love you I love you I love you
I love you I love you I love you I love you I love you I love you I love you
I love you I love you I love you I love you I love you I love you I love you
I love you I love you I love you I love you I love you I love you I love you
I love you I love you I love you I love you I love you I love you I love you
I love you I love you I love you I love you I love you I love you I love you
I love you I love you I love you I love you I love you I love you I love you
I love you I love you I love you I love you I love you I love you I love you
I love you I love you I love you

Here is, at this moment, what *Ariel* is thinking:

The band is called Computer.

We will perform in midsize venues all over the country and Europe, too.

VALLEY

At the floor of the valley in a deciduous environment where there are lupines and sunflowers and gerbera daisies you may now see a little girl, Valerie, sitting alone at a table with a red-and-white checkered cloth. The era was still sunset. There was still a soft breeze and the smell of a lake full of fish such as one called brown trout.

It is May of 2003. Little Valerie is seven years old, newly minted. Everyone in the whole world turned seven years old that year. Valerie is such a sweet girl, a profoundly happy child. She is not a very good student, but she is very funny and has a big imagination. And big eyes, big green eyes and brown hair that her mommy cut into a bob while little Valerie sat on the bathroom sink and on the toilet a slate-colored transistor radio played the hits from Mommy's childhood, a far-off land called 1972. And I don't even know how I knew any of this, but it was my special secret—the story of little Valerie.

Little Valerie, seven years old, newly minted, looked cute as a button, sitting there at her table on the floor of this valley that stretched for miles and miles.

"You have to play Patty-Cake Patty-Cake Baker's Man with little Valerie," said Ariel, who was standing next to me, listening to music on the ancient device they call Walkman. We were about one hundred feet away from little Valerie. She could not see us. So I walked over to her, crossing a field of cattails where at one point a stream kissed my feet and I saw a genuine frog and in the sky the soft drum of a chopper helicopter.

To my surprise, when I arrived, I was able to speak in a complete sentence for the first time in what felt like so long.

"Hi there, little Valerie," I said to the girl.

"Hiiii," she said.

"I am here to play Patty-Cake Patty-Cake Baker's Man with you, would you like that?"

"Very much," said little Valerie.

Little Valerie giggles and takes my hands. "Ontology is the study of the fundamental nature of Reality," said the birthday girl, with the biggest, happiest smile on her face. "And ontologically speaking," she continued, "I think you know exactly what is going on."

THUS SPOKE ZWEIG

TWENTY

Ariel was gone. The valley was gone, replaced by cherry oak walls, a moss green carpet, a halogen lamp on a bright red plastic end table. A girlfriend in a white shift dress with white daisies instructed me to once again take a seat. Dr. Altmann would be ready to see me shortly. I leaned back, cracked my knuckles, wiped my eyelids. I took a deep breath. On the intercom, Muzak. On a TV attached to the wall, silent footage of girlfriends playing tennis. Volley. Serve. Volley. Serve. I made a mental note to learn tennis.

I wondered what kind of sage advice Dr. Altmann would impart to me. Would he tell me to keep at it? Keep taking the drug? I was unsure. I was so weary. How long had I been here? There was so little I remembered about myself, why I had gotten the invite, what it was like back home. I just knew that more than ever I was closer to achieving my destiny. I was so close to being perfect.

I shivered. The room was growing colder and colder and when I closed my eyes I saw myself walking silently through a tundra, an archipelago, an autonomous archipelago, an autonomous archipelago. I remembered a time when it was always this quiet. When it was snow fluttering onto the roof of a clapboard house by a creek. And it used to be static in there—in my head. It was not always like this. It was not always loud.

The TV shut off. Then the music. A set of sliding doors opened, the girlfriend appeared again.

"Right this way, please," said the girlfriend.

The girlfriend approached the set of sliding doors and opened them. It was very dim in the room. There were no windows here. An electric fan buzzed softly. I was made to sit on a large beanbag chair. On the wall a flag blew in the artificial breeze. A light turned on. The flag was all white, except for black lettering, which just said: *ZWEIG*.

"Valerie Estelle," said a masculine voice.

I looked up. It was a pair of feet in a pair of cowboy boots attached to a powder blue suit. A genuine Stetson hat. I could not make out the face of the masculine voice, but I could see that he was reading *Girlfriend Weekly*.

"I trust you've enjoyed your time here. The girlfriends have spoken so highly of you and the progress you've made during your stay. Valerie Estelle. You're one of our sharpest candidates to date. We need to put you on the cover of *Girlfriend Weekly*. We need to get you on a goddamned waterslide. Fuck."

The masculine voice put down the magazine. It was Jethro! My water park agent!

"Sorry, do you mind if I eat some of this Big League Chew? Gets the blood vessels flowing. Mmm. You want some?"

I thought about it for a minute. Gum sounded awfully good right now and it would be wrong to be so rude and not accept such a thoughtful gift.

"Yes, please! I'll have some gum, and by the way, great to see you, Jethro. That is so crazy that you're also Dr. Zweig Altmann."

"Mmm. Yeah. Well. I'm a bag of mystery tricks. I've been following you for your whole life, chickadee. Let me tell you a little something. I'm a friend of your parents, you love all of our family photos. I'm your grandpapa, you love sitting on your grandpapa's lap. I'm your high school English teacher, you love fantasizing about sucking my cock while you read novels where the narrator is a girl who is caRazay. I'm your plumber, you love it when I fix your toilet. I'm your bank teller, you love it when I give you money, money, money, baby. I'm your water park agent, you love it when I fuck you in the back of my Charger after I shave your cunt with a pocketknife, meanwhile CDs are playing. I'm your boss when you're a cashier at the store, you love it when I make you organize the merchandise. I'm cosmic background microwave radiation, you love it when I'm the ionized gas that later condenses to make superclusters of galaxies. I'm a Boltzmann Brain sitting in a big fucking vat of green apple Jell-O (a Kraft Heinz product), you love that all of the memories of the universe exist for, like, thirty seconds tops before exploding in some kind of ergodic 'heat death.' I'm nobody, baby, you love how I am some kind of specter, haunting your life. You can't get rid of me. When you take that last big shit before you go to H-E-Double-Hockey-Sticks, I'll be floating over you, playing Johann Sebastian Bach on the bagpipes. I'll be waltzing 'The Blue Danube' on a collapsed star with some chick named Daphne M. Bernstein.

"Anyways, oh boy did I get sidetracked. You look so good. Drug's sure doing wonders on you. That's frontier psychiatry for you. Have you ever seen a horse run in slow motion over a peat bog? Been to Sarasota Jungle Gardens? Ever seen a macaw? Ever seen a wingspan so big you shit your pants? Your brain is like a singing saw, capable of a continuous glissando. *Continuous glissando.* Your brain's making you into an ideal chick for a son of God. Son of God. You look really slutty even with your bald head. You'd look fabulous in an outfit that's just tube socks and a genuine Stetson hat. Anyways. In an ideal world I'd hit you in the tit with a rolled-up newspaper. In an ideal world we'd put you in a talkie and dress you up like a Pierrot having a nosebleed. That's jazz, Valerie Estelle. That's a lonely drum kit crackling from electricity on one of the ninety-five moons of Jupiter. *As I was saying.*

"It's good to see you, and I'm happy to announce you've made it to the final stage of your test here at Mount Nothing regarding being one of the luckiest girls in the whole wide world. A perfect girlfriend! Now isn't that something. Here's what I want to do: I want you to come up here on this ten-thousand-dollar Danish teak desk that I bought on a website and spread your pussy lips out for daddy. Come on, sit on daddy's face. You're always so wet. No? I'm sensing a *no* from you based on your facial expressions. As you know, I'm perceptive. I'm the goddamn father of an experimental psychopharmaceutical company. They write articles about me in magazines! And also, I'd never have relations with a woman who wasn't hungry for my cock. I always could tell how badly you wanted it. I've seen you posing in my Charger in a bikini. I've seen you in Dead Horse Bay and you're like a trained seal doing that trick with the ball. I could always tell how badly you wanted it. You wanted it /so very badly/ didn't you? I would never make you do something you didn't want to do. Every man in the world has your best interests at heart. That's a little bit about why I got into medicine in the first place.

"Shall we proceed with the exam anyways? You have low blood pressure, that's lovely, Valerie Estelle. You have wonderful veins, that's lovely, Valerie Estelle. You have a little bit of cystic acne, Valerie Estelle. That's normal, Valerie Estelle. How many drinks would you say you have a week, on average? Between twenty and thirty? You naughty, naughty girl. Are you drunk right now? If you're not, we can fix that. Let's put you in a pair of pointe shoes and have you take so many shots of Fireball that you have to get your stomach pumped and then it is like a cartoon where your liver has googly eyes and starts reading a CDC pamphlet about how to just say no ☺☺☺.

"What was it that Ariel said when he taught you that very important lesson? Let's take a look at your file, shall we: *God, Reality, you need to stop getting wasted all the time, you're embarrassing me in front of all my friends.* Ah yes, and then once he said that he decided to fuck you! And you did such a good job, sweetheart! You lay there and you took it. And your brain produced for you a series of stunning images: of car fires and Potemkin villages and you are like Ann-Margret as Kim McAfee in your yellow dress shaking your ass on an Int'l Klein Blue Backdrop singing: *Conrad! You're A Gas!* But it's Ariel, not Conrad. What I'm trying to say is *you're gorgeous and I'm a genius.* Fuck. I'm gonna need an ice-cold American Coca-Cola. Where's My Girl Friday?"

Jethro/Zweig—I guess it would be more appropriate for me to call him my doctor and benefactor at this point—had moved from his chair and onto his desk. He was sitting there crouched like a praying mantis, hitting a little red button with the palm of his hand. "Girlfriend!" he yelled. "Ice-cold American Coca-Cola. And hurry up. I'm parched. It's like the Mongolian Gobi Desert in here."

The girlfriend from before came back in. She was on her hands and knees. She was naked. On her back was a little silver tray with a bottle of ice-cold American Coca-Cola.

"Hey, it's really nice to see you in this compromised position!" she said. "You now know me as the doctor's Girl Friday. Besides being a girlfriend, that's my profession."

"Hi, Girlfriend! I'm Girlfriend!" I said in a cheerful response. "I am Ariel's girlfriend, and I am awaiting further instructions about what to do next. You're totally cool."

"Well, that's seriously awesome. Let me know if you need a beverage such as a bottle of ice-cold American Coca-Cola! I'm not allowed to drink such precious elixirs and it would be an honor to serve you."

"Shut up, slut!" yelled the doctor, pulling a huge machine gun out of his Danish teak desk. "Get out of here!"

Girlfriend scampered off, remaining on her hands and knees at all times as the doctor fired his gun indiscriminately at the ceiling. I took my hands and plugged my ears. The loud noises were seriously making me freak out.

"Herr Doktor," I said. "You're seriously freaking me out."

"Sorry, babe, that's protocol," he said. "Anyways, darling girl, darling Valerie Estelle, tell me about your time here."

"Well," I said. "I've learned so much about myself as well as the way I function in large, community-oriented group spaces. I thrive when I get to use my creativity. For example, when I was made to act out Daphnis and Chloé, I enjoyed getting to pick out some pretty and very sparkly eyeshadow. Another thing I enjoyed was the more tactile work, such as doing handstands in the Atlantic Terminal Mall 2, even though this clearly is an area for improvement, as well as meeting little Valerie. Basically, I think I have ascended to the heights of a perfect girlfriend. Ariel will certainly be pleased. The way in which I completed these tasks was my signature sense of humor and, of course, my sex appeal."

"Fundamentally," said my doctor, "I'm gonna have to disagree. While I agree you did a stunning job with us, I did not like the way you just interacted with my Girl Friday. That was a test. I was testing you. That was way too convivial. That's not going to do. I expected better than that, especially coming from you. How, pray tell, can you be the best waterslide actress on the Eastern Seaboard and have that little tact when it comes to fraternizing with the enemy? Here's what I'm thinking. I'm going to count to one hundred and if you're still on the premises when I count to one hundred I'm going to take that machine gun you just saw me fire at the ceiling and point it into your asshole. Ipso facto, you will die a painful death from gun-related injuries. Sorry to get into an imbroglio, but that's the way it has to be, chickadee."

My brain was like an old TV stuck on a channel-search setting. I did not have a moment to spare. Here I was Reality Girlfriend Valerie running down the hallway. I broke into a gallop. The walls were now white, like a hospital. I heard music. I heard laughing. I galloped around the corner, it was a swerve that I did.

I stopped to catch my breath and opened a random door. There was no telling how close my doctor was to getting to one hundred. I really did feel like I was going to die here. It was not fair. I had so much life left in me. I took a deep breath.

Everything in this room was awash in blue. It was smoky. It was full of men wearing tuxedos. They were all smoking huge stogies. They were all drinking whiskey in highball glasses. It was so noisy with their speech. "Honey," said one of the men to me. "Happy New Year, gorgeous!"

The ceiling erupted in glitter and an elegant song began to play. The men all began to cheer. The men all finished their drinks. They closed in on me. I was drenched now in the blue lighting. They grabbed my wrists. They put me up against a dartboard. "We want to play a game to bring in the New Year!" they all shouted. One by one, the men lined up and took the darts and pointed them directly at my head. "The last time we did this," they all said, "it didn't really work out! The girl died so we cut off her arm and pinned it to the wall. It's over there if you want to see what we did!" I didn't, but I looked anyway. It was really gross.

There was a clock on the wall. One hundred seconds was probably almost here. In the distance, I heard the fluttering sound of discharged bullets, which you will recognize if you have ever heard a machine gun.

"I am so sorry, tuxedo men!!" I said. "I actually need you to let me go so I do not die at the hands of a pharmaceutical genius-cum-acting agent."

"But of course!" said the men.

"Goodbye! Adieu!" I said. "And Happy New Year!"

"If you want to leave," they said, "just walk through the stained-glass bar doors!"

Wow. It was cold in here. The next door had led to a fridge! Or was it a glacier? That would be nuts. There was nothing in here. There was no one in here. It was quiet, too. With the exception of the whipping winter winds. I could see the next door clearly. It was basically a straight shot. I was cold and I was afraid, but I knew that the mission was to keep going and that to stop would mean certain death. I looked up. A digital clock noted that out of one hundred seconds I was now down to fifteen. That wasn't a lot of time. I had to keep walking. It was so cold, but I had to keep walking.

The door swung open from the side that I had entered. It was my doctor. He had his machine gun. He was really prepared for the elements and had been outfitted with a fashionable parka and a pair of ski goggles.

"Twelve seconds, Valerie Estelle." He laughed. "That is not a lot of time."

"Eleven seconds," he said.

My walk turned into a sprint. My doctor started firing his gun. Ten seconds. It was not a lot of time. The door. I put my hand on the door. Using my brain and my hands I pulled on the door. I was going to make it. I was going to leave my doctor and Mount Nothing and I was going to find Ariel and be perfect for him and I was going to be good. I walked through the door and turned around. My doctor was directly behind me.

"You're on your own, kid. I guess I can't shoot you with my machine gun because you got out in time. But do not ask me for any favors. You could've become one of the luckiest girls in the world. You could've become a perfect girlfriend. Nope. Not today. Bye, little miss. And keep your phone on—think I might have work for you soon. New water park opening up in Schenectady County. That's upstate. Travel will be comped, obviously."

THUS SPOKE
THE VOICE

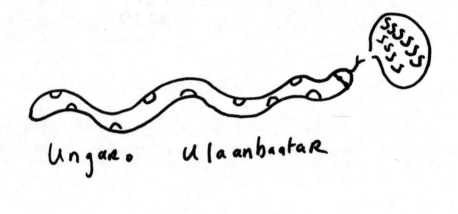

Ungaro   UlaanbaataR

TWENTY-ONE

I walked for miles. At one point there was a boat involved. When I first started walking I saw the occasional girlfriend tilling the land, but a strange thing was that as I walked farther and farther suddenly there was no one there. Not my boyfriend who was obsessed with the ancient device called Walkman, not my agent, Jethro, who was also a great scientific mind named Zweig Altmann. And it didn't even look like Lake Annecy 2 anymore. Everything had been replaced by miles and miles of lunar desert. Red rocks, cacti, white sands. A sky that was hot blue with no clouds. I looked down. A rare periwinkle garden snake wearing sunglasses slithered across my foot. It was the first living thing I had seen in so long. "Hi, snake," I said to the snake. "My name is Girlfriend." The snake continued slithering across my foot, then stopped and opened its little mouth.

"No, it'sssssss not," said the snake. "You can't lie to me, I'm a ssssss-nake in the dessssssert who can talk."

"Sorry, snake," I responded. "It's been kind of a strange journey. I've been walking for so long and there are no girlfriends left out here."

"That'sssss true," he said. "By the way, name issss Ungaro Ulaan-baatar."

"Hi, Ungaro Ulaanbaatar," I responded. "It's really nice to meet you."

"A pleassssssure. But there's no need to make sssssmall talk. I'm sssssure as hell you're trying to get back to Gowanussssssss so you can show your boyfriend that you're the greatest girlfriend of all time."

"Yeah!" I said.

"Ariel," said Ungaro Ulaanbaatar. "Honestly, weird pick for a boyfriend. I do not get the appeal of that guy. Gives off kind of a sssschool sssshooter vibe to me, but then again, I don't know much about human men. Momma sssay momma ssssah mom makusssa. I pretty much only fuck other rare periwinkle garden ssssnakessss wearing ssssunglassses. Anywaysssss. Here's the deal. It's pretty eassssssy actually. You jusssssst have to pull the sssssword from the ssssstone that is directly in front of the inverted Hollywood ssssign and then you're going to assssstral project into the Geneva airport and from there you'll be on a completely normal plane of exisssstence again and it will be very ssssstraightfor- ward in terms of getting home. A ticket hassss already been booked sssso you don't even need to worry about money. I'm warning you in advance—you're probably going to have to fly into Newark."

"Alright, that sounds good! Wait, what do you mean by *inverted Hollywood sign*?" I asked.

"Frankly, I've ssssaid too much. But I promisssssse you'll know it when you ssssssee it. I have to be on my way. Me and some of the other rare periwinkle garden ssssnakesss wearing ssssunglassses have planssss to throw down at the crapssss table later and I need to go home and put on sssssome cologne."

"Alrighty!" I said cheerfully. "It was nice to meet you, Ungaro Ulaan- baatar!"

"Yup," he responded. "Ok, bye."

I spent all day and all night walking through the desert. A thing about the desert that I didn't know is that it's sweltering hot during the day and pretty much ice-cold at night. Also there wasn't much in the way of water. I saw other rare periwinkle garden snakes wearing sunglasses after Ungaro Ulaanbaatar left me to go put on cologne and I thought about eating them but I was worried they were his friends so I didn't.

I wondered where Ariel had gone. I just wanted to show him that I was the greatest girlfriend of all time. But I guess I did not do a very good job. And it was of no matter here. It was pitch quiet. I was in the desert. It was just me and all of these rare periwinkle garden snakes wearing sunglasses. I could figure it all out when I got back to Gowanus. I could bake him a pie and tie his shoes. I could read him a storybook about a girl named Reality who knew all about the Assyrian Empire because she had a really smart boyfriend. I could have dinner with Ariel's mom and dad and laugh at their jokes. I could figure out how to make Ariel love me. I had learned his special lesson and I wasn't even that afraid of it the second time. I would do it again and again and again. I would even do it with a smile.

I kept moving. I followed the stars. The many billions of stars. And they were so big in the sky! I could see them so clearly. They looked like a basket of pearls. Or tiny little flecks of drugs that you will see if you are ever in Brooklyn and go to a DIY show at a place called Paradise (#221). It was really stunning. And so lonely. What did they do up there in those stars? I had some ideas. I took Intro to Astronomy in college.

Really what I wanted more than anything was to know if there was life out there and what all of that meant. Did they have boyfriends in outer space? Did girls named Reality do special tasks to prove their worth? I was unsure about this. But one thing I was sure about was that I needed a coat. It seemed like every step I got colder and colder.

My teeth started to chatter. I took a breath out of my mouth kind of as a test and noticed that when I did so I could see it like it was a big cloud or something.

"When she finally made it to the desert," said a voice, "the girl sighed like a baby bird."

I looked around. Was it Ungaro Ulaanbaatar already? No. It couldn't be him. I didn't recall him speaking of birds. After all, this voice had an authoritative tone.

"Imagine now," it said again, "that the wings are fluttering."

"I am doing this," I responded.

"Good," said the voice. "It's lovely to be in touch, Valerie. Or would you prefer Reality? Additionally: I know you're cold. I made a coat appear using my powers."

I looked around and saw that the voice had made a coat using its powers. It was leopard print and very large. I would bet money that it was made out of a bona fide dead leopard. I was not sure how to respond to the question about what name I'd like to be called so I just put on the coat and shivered.

"You're probably wondering who I am—I can't answer that. Nor can I tell you where the inverted Hollywood sign is. Basically, I'm the voice that has narrated your life over the course of the book. I am the all-seeing eye who has followed you on your journey to be the greatest girlfriend of all time."

"And I am grateful for this, All-Seeing Eye." I was instantly warm but could still see my breath.

"The girl melted into the ground," said the voice. "Imagine now in a nightmare scenario where if the girl does not sit on that rock over there chaos will ensue."

"Which one?" I asked. "There are, like, seventy-five million rocks."

Suddenly there was a lot of lightning. I guess I had made the voice angry. Apparently I was supposed to be a mind reader or something. I started to think that my life would be a trillion times better if I could do ESP.

"Stop thinking about what your life would be like if you had ESP. You don't have ESP. Ok, now listen. I'm now going to tell you some things. And you're not going to like them. First off—you're not the greatest girlfriend of all time. I guess you already knew that."

"I'm listening," I said, making myself comfortable on a large pile of rocks.

"You can try as hard as you want but you cannot force someone to love you. This is an impossible task. Ariel does not love you and you can't keep convincing yourself that the lesson will save your relationship. And the stuff with Katie? Jesus, that is going to be really devastating for you later. They're going to move in together after you break up—next to a women's shelter on Flatbush Avenue. But he'd never cheat on you. That's not his vibe. He hates dishonesty. Anyways, the Katie stuff is not the thing that will break your heart the most about Ariel. The thing that will break your heart the most about Ariel is that he never loved you, but he stayed with you anyways."

I took some more rocks and continued to pile them up. I wasn't sure why I was being lectured by some voice in the sky about my awesome boyfriend but whatever.

"You're not listening. I can see you. You're trying to make the largest rock sculpture in the world—that's not going to work. It already exists. Ever heard of Easter Island, chickadee? Pay attention. You could have fallen in love with anyone in the world. This is why you were able to go on this quest. Because, Valerie, Val, you have one of the most pure and open hearts in the world. Because 13.8 billion years ago particles burst into existence and a fireball exploded and a comet burst across the sky and in the Levant a girl found stone plates that said the words 'girlfriend' and 'weekly' and humanity shaped itself around the fact that it is possible to have a pure and open heart. And when someone is bold enough to have one of the most pure and open hearts in the world, they are bold enough to give it away to someone who will never love them back. This has been your destiny all along: to love incorrectly."

"Whatever."

"If you don't accept this TRUTH, you will be stuck here forever. You think that your love for him will be enough to sustain your relationship so you've deluded yourself into thinking that you can become the best girlfriend of all time by enrolling in a psychopharmacological study. And I hate to break it to you but the stuff in ZZZZvx Ultra is basically just the growth hormone they give to cows so that they are always ready to give some milk. That's why you've been lactating. Accept this TRUTH! Live in the NOW! Focus! I'm going to create a huge gust of wind so that your rock sculpture falls over. Ok, bye—I have to go throw down at the craps table. Voices from the sky are also friends with rare periwinkle garden snakes wearing sunglasses."

Suddenly, a tornado appeared and it knocked over my sculpture. I was still so cold! And I was really struggling. Jesus. I was seriously feeling like Wile E. Coyote when he gets absolutely killed by the dastardly Road Runner courtesy of some ACME dynamite. The voice from the sky was onto something, I guess. I might as well accept what it said. Especially because I didn't want to be trapped in the cold desert, especially since my rock sculpture had been destroyed.

But I wasn't ready to give up. I had to at least try one last time.

I looked up. The night sky was turning mauve, the stars were fading into the horizon line. I could feel it getting warmer, so I peeled off my bona fide leopard jacket. I was starting to bake so I took off all of my clothes. In front of me I saw the sign. But it didn't say HOLLYWOOD. It said YOLO.

Ungaro Ulaanbaatar was right. I *did* know it when I saw it. And the beauty was unimaginable. Picture the most beautiful thing you've ever seen, for example a baby being bornth or a kindness that is feral and pure or a shooting star or seven dogs standing watch in front of a remote cabin and it has nothing on seeing a huge sign in the middle of the desert when the sun is beginning to rise and you are naked and the words that the sign says proclaim the truest and bluest expression of all time: *YOU ONLY LIVE ONCE!*

But where was the sword in the stone? Wasn't that a key part of the puzzle? I turned around. Oh! There it was!!! I found it!! It was a big hunk of red desert rock and in the center of it was a beautiful golden sword which featured many gemstones including opals, emeralds, sapphires, rubies, amethysts, and peridots. I hoped that once I freed it from the rock I'd get to take it home to show Ariel.

I took a deep breath. Grrrghghhhhhhh uggggghh. Agh!! This was pretty hard. I'm not sure if you've ever had to pull a jewel-encrusted golden sword from a huge chunk of red desert rock but let me tell you: it's really hard. Like, harder than opening a jar of pasta sauce or trying to move a car that has sorrowfully ran out of gas on a country road in the Southern Adirondacks while it is in neutral. I tried again. Agghghhhhh AAAAHHHHH PFFRRRRFFFF GAHHHH!!!!!!!!!!! Ok, no dice. I was starting to get seriously pissed off at Ungaro Ulaanbaatar for

YOLO

(just like the
Hollywood Sign)

giving me such garbage advice. Maybe I just needed to think of Ariel's shining face. I pictured Ariel's shining face. For context, it was his face when one time on Rockaway Beach at around Beach 110th Street we bought nutcrackers and he drank his too fast and got kind of drunk and developed this horny and adorable stare. I pulled again. AGHHH-HHH eeeeeeeeFFFFFFF!!! Fuck. It didn't work. Maybe I had to picture my former friends Soo-jin and Lord Byron. I did this and imagined all of us eating at Tashkent Buffet World, laughing. I pulled.

PPPPPPPPPFDSGHLFGJDKSDFGKHGSDFKLGHDF. JESUS CHRIST!!! I couldn't do it. I tried the same thing with Emil. With my parents. With Stefie. No dice. No dice!

I was about to literally kill myself by punching myself in the face. I didn't know what to do! Why hadn't any of these mystical forces in the desert given me better advice other than "you will recognize the sign" and "you have a pure and open heart."

I had an idea. I closed my eyes and approached the sword in the stone. I took a deep breath and imagined myself playing a winning game of solitaire in an amazing outfit. Suddenly, the sword loosened. I pulled it out of the rock like it was a piece of gum from a gum holder. The sword glowed even more brilliantly than before. It had clearly been, like, four hours or something since I started because now the midday sun was casting a stunning glow.

Ungaro Ulaanbaatar was on the rock! He was here to congratulate me, certainly.

"I had some lossssssssssses in my game of crapssss but it was worth it because I finally got to take my new cologne for a ssspin," said my rare periwinkle garden snake wearing sunglasses friend. "Also congratssss."

"Thanks," I said. "But why did I have to picture myself playing a winning game of solitaire in order to retrieve the sword from the stone instead of a cherished memory?"

Ungaro Ulaanbaatar stuck out his little tongue in contemplation and then said:

"Exissssstence is meaninglesssssssss and random. YOLO."

WE COME TO
THE END

When she finally got dumped by her boyfriend, the girl sighed like a baby bird. *Imagine now that the wings are fluttering.* The girl melted into the ground. *Imagine now in a nightmare scenario where she comes home after a long trip and the boy is just sitting on the couch alone drinking a beer.* Her eyes welled up with tears. *Imagine now that this is because he cared about her, but not in a way that involves long-term commitment.* She fell to her knees. *It's just that I'm almost twenty-seven,* he said. *I can't stay with someone I don't see a future with.* And then he begged her to stay, just one more night.

Due to all of the above, there was some talk of leaving the apartment and going home and drowning herself in the bathtub.

She was calm in her explanation of why she should go home and drown herself in the bathtub. "I gave you a year of my life," she said. "I never even told you that I loved you and now you're breaking up with me. Please don't do this."

The girl was acting like this for a really normal reason, actually. The reason is that she had arrived at a moment in her quest where she had realized it was one giant failure. And when you realize your quest was one giant failure you have a thought that is like: Well, what was the point of all of this?

So the girl stayed over and did the only natural thing in this situation which was that she had sex with the boy in his bed. And she could not stop crying the whole time and the boy asked if she could keep it down while he was trying to eat her ass. He really wanted to make her cum and it was hard to focus when you cry like that. When they were done fucking they both fell asleep.

The next morning, when she woke up, the girl decided to put the finishing touches on a zine she had made about their time together. She decided to call it *Paradise Logic*. Because of Paradise (#221), the DIY venue. But also because of Paradise in the classical sense. Paradise as in back rows of the theater. Paradise as in the gods, the corner of the sky where you are closest to Olympus, kissing the rings of heaven. Paradise as in where they sat the poor people at a play. Because when you are twenty-three you will slum it for love. You will sit in the back row on purpose. You will live in a dumpster and sleep on top of newspaper and fall in love with a boy who is named Ariel. You will meet him at a punk venue and he will take you on a first date where you play pinball and do kissing. You will say: I know this is bad. And yet. *And yet.* Life can be very beautiful when you squint hard from the shit seats, in that place called Paradise. Especially when you are age twenty-three and every terrible thing you do feels remarkable. Every terrible thing you do puts you one inch closer to the gods.

She wrote the name down on a piece of paper. It looked perfect.

And then she put the zine on his nightstand and then she left. Because there was still one last final leg of her quest: to go to work. And to get to work she had to walk. So she walked past the glittering waters of the Gowanus where one time Ariel had told her she was beautiful totally beautiful and the bodegas on Third Avenue where one time Ariel had protected her from the terrible cat Noor and the new nightclub that had just opened up where one time Ariel had purchased her a cocktail and touched her breasts and the head shops on Pacific where one time Ariel had purchased her the gift of weed and a cup of coffee from the halal cart where one time Ariel had held her hand.

And the early morning light was mauve and it was the first cold day of the year so she shivered and the drunks stumbled out of their bars and it did feel like fifteen million cats were on parade and sometimes

PARADISE
LOGIC

your life is ruled by cowboys in powder blue suits and according to lizards in the desert, existence was meaningless and random but that did not mean that it could not also be beautiful, stunning to be alive, *alive* (alive, alive, alive). And one thing about Ariel is he had a freckle on his eyelid and another thing was it was true that he was once a child genius of the piano and at its best it was a taxi ride across the Brooklyn Bridge with the windows down in pollen season featuring a drum machine loop, the electrical charge of a streetlamp and the dissemination of snow and you are giddy when a song explodes into a brass section at its midpoint and at its worst it was so scary, it was so scary, it was so scary, it was so scary, and when she reached her place of business she went down the escalator and the grounds of the Atlantic Terminal Mall were certainly not fallow.

And the cold shower in the locker room was a divinity and the mole in between her breasts looked like it was winking at her and the girl's uniform fit her so perfectly and the customers on the floor, the few of them that there were at Lids this early in the morning, they idled in front of the hundreds of thousands of millions of baseball caps, a constellation of baseball caps, and the girl smiled because she was already useful and sometimes an antidote to sadness is being given a task and when she scanned the barcode the thoughts cracked open in her brain like the great big egg and they were like:

Did you find everything you were looking for today?

And then:

Did it make you walk toward the light?

IT DID

IT REALLY DID

YOLO

ACKNOWLEDGMENTS

Thank you to my agent, Jim Rutman, for your excellent guidance, and for believing in my weird little book. I am so grateful to have you in my corner. Thank you also to everyone else at Sterling Lord Literistic, especially Christopher Combemale. Thank you to my editors, Olivia Taylor Smith and Sophie Missing, for helping me to sharpen my vision, and for advocating and encouraging me to push myself at every step of the way. Thank you to everyone at Simon & Schuster and Scribner UK, especially Brittany Adames, Martha Langford, and Ella Fox-Martens, for showing so much care and consideration toward my project. And of course to Martha Kennedy for the perfect cover.

To Sally Singer, for *Vogue* and telling me to go to grad school. Thank you for being a wonderful friend and mentor.

To Daniel Kolitz, for telling me about every cool book ever written and then suggesting that I "try writing a short story some time." You were never Ariel.

To Andy Fidoten, for reading my book countless times and being the most diligent, perfect reader ever. I could not have done this without you.

To my Columbia professors: Sam Lipsyte, Ben Marcus, Gary Shteyngart, Adam Wilson, Jen George, and Jean Kyoung Frazier.

To Daniel Arnold, for the beautiful photos.

To my friends, many of whom read many early versions of this book: Dani Blum, Silas Jones, Claudia Ross, Vrinda Jagota, Samantha Adler, Anika Jade Levy, Sophie Madeline Dess, Megan Nolan, Mateo Rispoli, Anthony Ashley, William Hutton, Julian Meltzer, Sage Vousé,

Cella Wright, Lyris Faron, Dena Miller, Arielle Gordon, Sarah Conner, Bryn Weiler, and Jules Darmanin.

Lastly, to my family. Thank you for giving me the experience of something as crazy as being loved from the moment I entered this world, just like Reality.

ABOUT THE AUTHOR

SOPHIE FRANCES KEMP was born in 1996 in Schenectady, New York. Her fiction and essays have appeared in *Granta*, *The Paris Review*, *Vogue*, *GQ*, *Pitchfork*, and *The Baffler*, among others. She received her MFA in fiction at Columbia University, where she now teaches in the writing program. She lives in Brooklyn.